Hawaiian Tales

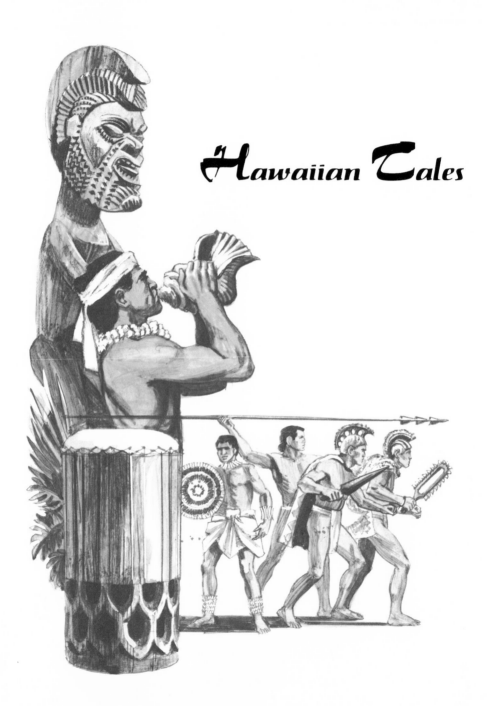

Hawaiian Tales

Vivian L. Thompson

of Heroes and Champions

illustrated by
Herbert Kawainui Kane

Holiday House, New York

Text copyright © 1971 by Vivian L. Thompson
Illustrations copyright © 1971 by Herbert Kawainui Kane
All rights reserved
Printed in the United States of America
Library of Congress Catalog Card Number: 72–151757
ISBN 0–8234–0192–8

to KRH
who knows why

Contents

Foreword

THE PEOPLE OF Old Hawaii had their unique heroes and champions, and many of these were kupua, or supernatural. Some were shape-shifters, like Shark Man of Ewa who could change from man to shark to rat to a bunch of bananas. Some had extraordinary powers, like Kana the stretching kupua who could stretch himself as tall as a palm tree, as slender as a bamboo, as thin as a morning glory vine, as fine as a spider web. Others had rare weapons, like Palila's flying war club, Ka-ui-lani's talking spear, Pikoi's magic arrows. To these were added gods in human form, like Ku-ula, god of fishing; and children of the gods, like Aiai who used his father's enchanted talismans to develop an early ecological program.

Whatever form he took, the kupua was a way of explaining the unexplainable. As in all tales told and retold by word of mouth, change and exaggeration creep in. Perhaps this is how the kupua tale developed, through exaggeration. That it has survived and continues to entertain is an indication of its universal appeal.

Here then, are twelve such tales—kupua tales of Old Hawaii.

January, 1971   —VIVIAN L. THOMPSON

The Stretching Kupua

ONCE IN OLD HAWAII, in the days when anything was possible, there was born to Hina-the-Beautiful a kupua child named Kana. Following the custom for high-born first sons, Kana was given to his grandparents to be reared.

Grandmother Uli, herself a sorceress, laid the child on a bed of kapa mats and built above it a shelter of lehua boughs and sweet-smelling maile vines. She fed the child for forty days and it grew forty feet. As it grew she enlarged the shelter. By the time Kana was fully grown, his hale stretched from the mountain to the sea.

Being forty feet tall might have disturbed some. It bothered Kana not at all, for he knew that if he ever needed to be taller, he had the special kupua power of stretching himself as tall as a palm tree, as slender as a bamboo, as thin as a morning glory vine, as fine as a spider web.

Later, a younger brother, Niheu, was born but Kana saw little of him for he was reared by his mother.

The years passed and Kana grew into a mild-mannered youth. He owned a powerful club which he seldom used, for his favorite occupations were eating and sleeping. When he ate, forty calabashes of poi made his meal. When he slept, the mountain shook with his snores.

One fine day when Kana was enjoying his mid-morning nap, he heard a faint call.

"Kana! Wake up!"

"Go away," Kana mumbled. "I am busy."

"Kana! There is trouble! Big trouble!"

Grumbling, Kana sat up and looked about. Down at his feet stood his normal-sized brother, Niheu, hands cupped to mouth, calling up to him.

"What is this big trouble, Small Brother?" Kana asked, yawning.

"Chief Kauila has carried off Hina, our mother!"

"Which Kauila?"

"Kauila-the-Dauntless of Haupu Hill!"

"Oh. That Kauila." Kana nodded and his eyes began to close. They soon opened when he felt a stinging. His brother was chopping at his great toe with his axe.

"Wake up, Kana!" Niheu cried. "Kauila has carried her off to the island of Molokai. We must go after her!"

"No trouble," Kana replied. "Get me a canoe."

Niheu ran off. Only a very special canoe would carry his giant brother. He summoned the island's canoe-makers and told them what was needed. They went into the forest, chose a great koa tree seven feet across, and made a canoe.

News of these preparations reached the island of Molokai. Kauila's advisor, Moi, brought a warning.

"O Chief, return this woman! I have dreamed a dream. I saw a great canoe bringing the woman's kinsmen to destroy you!"

Kauila smiled. "Moi, forget your dream. No man of Hawaii is brave enough to attack Kauila-the-Dauntless!"

Next day Moi stood before Kauila again. "O Chief, return this woman! I have dreamed a second dream. On our own royal beach I saw footprints six feet long! Footprints of a giant who comes to destroy you!"

Kauila scoffed. "Moi, forget your dream. No man lives with feet so large."

A third time Moi brought a warning. "O Chief, I have dreamed once more. I followed the footprints and behold! They were made by a giant as tall as Haupu Hill! You must return this woman!"

Kauila scowled. "Moi, enough of your dreams! You forget that Haupu Hill is an enchanted hill. I can make it rise until its summit is lost in the clouds. I will not return Hina!"

Back on the island of Hawaii, Niheu reported to Kana that the canoe was ready. Kana picked up his club, strode to the launching place, and stepped into the canoe.

Crack! His foot broke through the flooring and down went the canoe.

"No trouble," said Kana. "I shall make another canoe."

He reached into the forest, found a koa tree ten feet across, and uprooted it. He chopped it into shape with his hands, hollowed it out with his fingernails, and set it in the water. Then with fourteen paddlers, the great canoe set out. Niheu steered. Kana slept. But not for long.

"Kana! Wake up!" cried Niheu. "What a time for sleeping! Kauila has blown us aground on a rocky ledge!"

"No trouble," said Kana. He picked up his club, leaned out and struck the rocky ledge a mighty blow. The ledge shattered. The canoe slid free. Kana went back to sleep. But not for long.

"Kana! Wake up!" cried Niheu. "What a time for sleeping!

Kauila has sent a mountainous wave to swamp our canoe!"

"No trouble," said Kana. He picked up his club, leaned forward and struck the wave a mighty blow. The wave split in two. The canoe passed through. Kana went back to sleep. But not for long.

"Kana! Wake up!" cried Niheu. "What a time for sleeping! Kauila has sent a monstrous fish to eat us alive!"

What did Kana say? What he always said. "No trouble." He picked up his club, leaned backward and struck the monstrous fish a mighty blow. It sank from sight. The canoe went on. But Kana did not go back to sleep. Who could enjoy sleeping with all these petty interruptions?

Soon the island of Molokai came in sight, and on it, a tall rounded hill. "Behold!" cried Niheu. "High on that hill lives Kauila-the-Dauntless! It is there he has taken our mother."

"No trouble," said Kana. "We shall catch him by surprise. Leave the paddlers here with me. You seek out this Kauila. When you have found him, call me and I shall finish him off."

Grumbling, Niheu set out along the rocky beach. His foot slipped and caught between two rocks. He wrenched it free and ran back.

"Kana, listen!" he cried. "Kauila has set traps among the rocks! He caught me in one and I barely managed to get free!"

"No trouble," said Kana. "Take the sandy trail."

Sighing, Niheu set out along the sandy beach. He stooped down to watch some sand crabs digging their holes and got sand thrown in his eyes. Rubbing them, back he ran.

"Kana, listen!" he cried. "Kauila's men are hiding in holes along the beach! They threw sand in my eyes and nearly blinded me!"

"No trouble," said Kana. "Take the forest trail."

Groaning, Niheu set out once more. Up the forest trail he climbed. Two seabirds swooped overhead on their way to the sea. With arms wrapped about his head, back ran Niheu.

"Kana, listen!" he cried. "Kauila has two giant birds guarding his hill. They attacked me in the forest! I was lucky to escape with my life!"

Kana shook his head. "Stay here with the paddlers, Niheu," he said. "I will go."

Up the forest trail strode Kana. But as he climbed, the hill began rising into the blue sky.

"Ho, Kauila! Two can play that trick," said Kana. Then, using his kupua stretching power, he stretched himself tall as a palm tree. Up went Kana . . . up went the hill. He stretched himself slender as a bamboo. Up went Kana . . . up went the hill. He stretched himself thin as a morning glory vine. Up went Kana . . . up went the hill.

Then Kana took a deep breath and stretched himself fine as a spider web. Now he could see the top of the hill just above him, and on it the home of the Molokai chief. But auwe! Kana had stretched himself so thin that he had no strength left to face Kauila-the-Dauntless!

At his feet far below, Niheu called a message, but a day and a night passed before the words reached Kana.

"Stretch yourself back to our island and ask Grandmother Uli to feed you!"

Kana nodded. He stretched himself back to Hawaii, poked his head through the doorway of his grandmother's hale, and in a weak voice asked for food.

Grandmother Uli provided food—a netful of fish . . . a kalo patchful of pounded poi . . . an ovenful of baked pig.

Kana ate hungrily and felt his strength returning. Then satisfied, he closed his eyes and slept. But not for long.

"Kana! Wake up!" cried Grandmother Uli. "What a time for sleeping! Your brother is waiting! Your mother is weeping!"

"No trouble," said Kana. "Now that I am strong again I shall reach the top of Haupu Hill and make short work of Kauila-the-Dauntless."

"Not so fast," said Grandmother Uli. "One thing you should know. Haupu Hill is no ordinary hill. It is really a giant turtle. Only one thing can stop its rising. You must find its flippers and break them off. Then it can rise no higher."

Kana nodded, then gave a yelp. The day before, impatient Niheu, back on Molokai, had begun chopping at Kana's foot with his axe. Now Kana felt some discomfort.

"I'm coming! I'm coming!" Kana roared. Bidding a hasty farewell to Grandmother Uli, he stretched himself back to the island of Molokai.

As soon as he came near, the hill began rising again. Kana looked about and found the first flipper. With one mighty stamp of his right foot he broke it off.

The hill rose more slowly. Kana looked about and found the second flipper. With one mighty stamp of his left foot he broke that off. The hill came to a halt.

Kana gave one last long stretch and reached the summit of Haupu Hill. There stood Hina, his beautiful mother, smiling through her tears. There stood Kauila-the-Dauntless, shivering and shaking at the sight of this giant who had overtaken him on his enchanted hill.

With his right hand, Kana picked up Kauila and tossed him far out into the sea. With his left, he picked up his beautiful mother, bent down, and set her gently in the canoe.

"Niheu will take you home, my mother," he said. "I have a small task to finish."

When the canoe was safely at sea, Kana gave a mighty stamp

with both feet. Haupu Hill shattered into a hundred pieces. Each piece fell into the water and became a small turtle swimming away in fright.

Then mild-mannered Kana stretched himself back to the island of Hawaii, back to his normal size of forty feet, back to his hale that stretched from the mountain to the sea, back to his interrupted nap.

The Flying War Club

PALILA WAS PART MAN, part spirit, raised by his guardian in Ala-na-po, temple of the gods, and highly trained in the use of the war club. When he was grown, he said to his guardian, "Enough of practice and drilling, Makua. It is time to go out in the world and make use of the skill you have given me."

His guardian nodded. "Ae, it is time. But remember this, Palila. Use your skill for good, not evil. Help the good resist the evil."

"I will remember," Palila promised.

"Then here is a magic war club. Twirl it and it will carry you wherever you would go. Wield it in a good cause and it will bring you victory."

Palila thanked his guardian. Twirling the club, he pointed it before him, and clinging to its handle was carried swiftly to the island of Oahu.

Now at this time, the island was ruled by High Chief Ahu-a-pau, a man of exalted rank. The sun was not permitted to shine upon him, the rain to fall upon him, nor the wind to blow upon him. On going out, he went in a covered litter carried by two swift runners. In this manner he traveled the length and breadth of his island. But there were two districts he did not visit—Ewa and Ko-o-lau.

Word of the arrival of a warrior with a flying war club soon reached the high chief's advisor. He sent for Palila and after questioning him, presented him to Ahu-a-pau, saying:

"This is Palila, son of the gods,
Reared in the temple of Ala-na-po.
Palila of the flying war club.
Palila who offers his services."

Ahu-a-pau smiled a crafty smile. "Welcome, Palila," he said. "I can use such a warrior. I have a small problem in the district of Ewa. Some mysterious force is carrying off my people who swim in the bay there."

Palila thought of his guardian's words: help the good resist the evil. Swimmers against a mysterious evil force? A worthy cause.

Ahu-a-pau, seeing Palila hesitate, added slyly, "I have two fair daughters. The man who solves this problem for me may have the daughter of his choice. Would you care to try?"

"I would," said Palila, and off he flew to Ewa.

There, he started down the road to the bay and soon came to a small farm and a farmer leaning on his digging stick. He was sleek and well-fed, and though the day was warm, wore a kapa shoulder cape.

"Greetings," said Palila. "Is swimming good in the bay?"

"Excellent," said the farmer. "I have never known better."

"Will you join me?"

"Auwe," the farmer answered, "I have no time for swimming." He set to work with his digging stick. Palila continued on down

the winding road to a rocky ledge overlooking the bay. The blue water lay calm and undisturbed.

Down a footpath from the rear of the farm, Palila saw the farmer come running. Moving out of sight, Palila rolled a stone into the water with a splash; saw the farmer race to the edge and dive.

Peering from his hiding place, Palila saw no sign of a swimmer —saw only the ugly fin of a shark; a shark with a broad brown band across its back, circling . . . circling. . . .

As Palila watched, the shark disappeared. Soon, up the rocky ledge climbed the farmer, water dripping from shoulder cape and malo. Scowling, he took the footpath back to his farm.

Then Palila dived in, enjoyed a refreshing swim, and climbed the winding road to the farm again. There he saw so sign of the farmer, but on the rock wall crouched a huge gray rat with a broad brown band across its back, its beady eyes watching him.

Palila struck at the rat with his club . . . it jumped, squealing, into a banana tree. Palila swung at the tree . . . the rat turned into a bunch of bananas. Palila swung at the fruit . . . it changed back into a rat that leaped to the ground and darted behind the farmer's house.

Palila gave chase. Around the corner he ran. There was no sign of the rat but the farmer stood there, smiling. "Greetings," he said. "Did you enjoy your swim?"

"I did indeed," Palila answered. "Did you enjoy yours?"

"I told you I have no time for swimming," the farmer said crossly.

"So you did, yet your clothes are wet."

"Oh, that." The farmer shrugged. "I watered my field."

Palila nodded. "You should take off your wet clothes. Let me help you with your cape."

"No! No!" There was a note of terror in the farmer's voice. "I was just about to change." He hurried into his house.

Palila's face was thoughtful. He made his way to the overseer of the district and said, "I am here on the chief's business. I believe this man who pretends to be a farmer is a shark-man, one who can change his form at will. Here is what you should do."

The overseer called out a work party. All able-bodied men were ordered to report for work. The farmer, still wearing his cape, appeared with the others. Palila whispered to the overseer.

The overseer spoke. "There is hard work to be done, and the day is warm. Wear malo only."

Up and down the line, men threw off any extra clothing. All but the farmer. He pretended not to hear. Then, as the overseer started toward him, he broke from the line and ran.

Palila stretched out his club. The farmer went sprawling. As he fell, his shoulder cape flew up, revealing upon his back the fierce jaws of a shark.

With angry cries the men fell upon the shape-shifter. No more would he shift from man to shark. No more would he feed on their neighbors, their kinsmen, their children.

Palila flew back to Chief Ahu-a-pau. "I have come to report," he said. "The waters of the bay are safe for swimming. The Shark Man of Ewa is no more."

"Good! Good!" said Ahu-a-pau, rubbing his hands. "Now I can swim in Ewa bay without fear of harm." Seeing Palila's expression change he added, "Oh yes, my daughters." Soon they appeared: one small and dainty, one tall and stately.

"Which do you choose?" asked the chief.

Palila, seeking adventure, not marriage, hesitated. "How could a man choose between two such fair daughters?" he asked. "I would have to take both."

The high chief gulped. "Ah yes . . . not a choice to be made lightly. Perhaps another adventure first?"

"Another adventure," Palila agreed generously.

Ahu-a-pau rubbed his hands together and smiled his crafty smile. "What can I offer to tempt a man of your talent? Let me see. . . . Ah yes, the district of Ko-o-lau. A fellow named Olomano has been doing away with my people who travel through the district."

Palila considered. Innocent travelers against a murderous outlaw? A worthy cause.

While Palila hesitated, Ahu-a-pau cast about for a suitable bribe. "The man who could rid us of this outlaw would be worthy to ride in my own royal litter. Would you care to try?"

"I would," said Palila, and off he flew to Ko-o-lau. There he came upon a woman weeping by the roadside and asked why she wept.

"My husband," she sobbed. "His overseer sent him on an errand and he has not returned. I fear the wicked Olomano has killed him."

"I shall find out," said Palila, and started off.

"Take care!" cried the woman. "This Olomano is stronger than any man you have ever met."

Palila nodded and went on his way. Soon he came to an old man peering into the distance, and asked what he sought.

"My son," said the man. "He went fishing and has not returned. I fear the wicked Olomano has killed him."

"I shall find out," said Palila, and started off.

"Take care!" called the old man. "This Olomano is bigger than any man you have ever met."

Palila nodded and went on his way. Soon he met a young boy running toward him and asked why he ran.

"My brother!" cried the boy. "We were walking through the woods and the wicked Olomano caught him! Now he is coming after me!"

"Let him catch me instead," said Palila, and started off.

"Take care!" shouted the boy. "This Olomano is more terrible than any man you have ever met."

Palila nodded and went on his way. How people exaggerated. What could go wrong on such a day? The sky was sunny. Mild breezes blew. Birds sang in the trees.

Then without warning, the sun was blotted out. The breezes died. The birds hushed their song. Through the sudden stillness came a roaring voice. "Who dares trespass on the land of Olomano?"

Ahead of him, Palila saw what had blotted out the sun and shut off the breezes—the warrior Olomano, thirty-six feet tall and broad as a house.

One glance told Palila it would be useless to attack such a foe from the ground. Twirling his club, he pointed it high, sailed through the air, and landed lightly on the giant's left shoulder.

Olomano gave a bellow of rage. "Who dares touch the shoulder of Olomano?"

Palila made reply:

"I am Palila, son of the gods,
Reared in the temple of Ala-na-po.
Palila of the flying war club,
Palila who exposed Shark Man of Ewa,
Palila, slayer of the giant Olomano."

The giant gave a mighty laugh—a laugh he never finished—for Palila raised his magic war club and cleaved Olomano in two.

Then Palila twirled his mighty war club and flew back the way he had come. On the steep path below, he saw the high chief's royal litter and flew down to meet it. At sight of him the runners stopped, the chief poked out his head.

"I have come to report," said Palila. "The district of Ko-o-lau is safe again. The giant Olomano is no more."

"Excellent! Excellent!" said Ahu-a-pau, rubbing his hands. "Now I may ride through the length and breadth of the island in safety."

"And I may ride in your royal litter," said Palila.

Chief Ahu-a-pau smiled weakly. "But you, who travel by swift flying war club, would be impatient with the slower pace of a litter, eh?"

Palila nodded. "Ae, I would. But I would control my impatience to help a high chief keep his word." He moved a step closer.

Slowly, sullenly, High Chief Ahu-a-pau climbed from his royal litter and gave Palila his place. Palila called an order and the runners started off.

Looking back, Palila saw the exalted High Chief Ahu-a-pau trudging up the steep path to his royal dwelling, out in the open where the sun could shine upon him, the rain fall upon him, the wind blow upon him, like any common man.

At the top of the hill, Palila called the runners to a halt and climbed out. He had used his skill for the good of Ewa swimmers and Ko-o-lau travelers, and he was glad of that. He had hoped to help a concerned chief as well, but had helped only a vain and selfish one. High Chief Ahu-a-pau? He had seen enough of him. Twirling his club, he pointed it before him and off he flew to the island of Hawaii.

Landing at Hilo, he heard of warfare between Chief of Hilo and Chief of Hamakua.

"Who is winning?" he asked.

"Chief of Hamakua," he was told. "His forces are far superior in every way."

"A worthy cause," said Palila and straightway presented himself to the losing chief and offered his services.

Chief of Hilo accepted eagerly but being a man of rare honesty, said, "I must warn you. We have little chance of winning. My opponent has in his army the renowned Three Warriors of Hamakua, whose name strikes terror in the hearts of my bravest men."

"It strikes no terror in mine," Palila replied. "I can win the victory for you. Here is what we shall do."

The two went forth to meet the enemy and Chief of Hilo called out, "Chief of Hamakua! Send forth your best warrior against my best. Let these two decide our struggle."

Chief of Hamakua made arrogant reply. "My best warrior? Ka! I have three best warriors!

"Send all three," Palila answered.

Third Warrior stepped forth, jabbing and thrusting with a wicked short spear.

"Auwe!" whispered the men behind Palila. "It is said his spear tore the great hole in the cliff at Onomea!"

Palila nodded pleasantly.

Second Warrior stepped forth, brandishing a long spear of tremendous proportions.

"Auwe!" muttered the men behind Palila. "It is said his spear once pierced a rain cloud and flooded the island!"

Palila smiled politely.

First Warrior stepped forth, twirling a gigantic knobbed war club, the like of which no one had ever seen.

"Auwe!" groaned the men behind Palila. "It is said his club struck the ground and gouged out Waipio Valley!"

Palila yawned slightly, then he stepped forth.

"These are your best, O Chief of Hamakua?" he asked. "No matter. If you have no better, these must do."

"Who is this arrogant young cock?" Chief of Hamakua demanded.

Palila answered:

"I am Palila, son of the gods,
Reared in the temple of Ala-na-po.
Palila of the flying war club,
Palila who exposed Shark Man of Ewa,
Palila, slayer of the giant Olomano,
Palila, slayer of the Three Warriors of Hamakua."

Chief of Hamakua gave a scornful laugh. "When my Three Warriors have finished with you I shall hang your clacking jaws from the nearest tree!"

"Try," said Palila.

"Begin!" cried Chief of Hamakua. The three stepped forward, Third Warrior jabbing and thrusting with his short spear, Second Warrior brandishing his long spear, First Warrior twirling his gigantic war club.

Palila stood motionless until the three were nearly upon him. Then he swung his club, up . . . down . . . across . . . and killed all three.

Wrenching the jaws from each, he presented them to Chief of Hamakua. "You may still have your Tree of the Clacking Jaws, my friend. Here is not one set but three, and yours will make four!"

So saying, Palila swung his club again and that was the end of Chief of Hamakua, and the end of Palila's adventures.

The Talking Spear

KA-UI-LANI WAS HIS NAME, son of High Chief Kea-hua, born high in the forest at Place-of-Many-Waters on the island of Kauai. He was raised by his father's parents, far from his birthplace, and bathed in a sacred stream whose waters caused him to grow rapidly.

When he was fully grown, he set out to see his parents, no easy journey back to Place-of-Many-Waters. There he was welcomed warmly by his father and a small group of followers.

Greetings over, Ka-ui-lani asked, "How is it, my father, that you, a high chief, live in this deserted spot with so few followers?"

Chief Kea-hua's face grew sad. "It was not always so, my son. Once I was the most powerful chief on the island of Kauai, with vast lands and many forties of warriors. But before you were born, a sea kupua, Akua-of-the-Swollen-Billows, destroyed my lands, killed my warriors, and sent your mother and me and a few faithful followers fleeing to these forest uplands beyond his reach. Here I have waited for the day you would come to avenge me."

"And I have come," said Ka-ui-lani, "but how am I to destroy such a powerful enemy with so few men?"

"There is a way, my son. See this." His father led him to a spear rack holding a single heavy spear of polished wood. "When I was young and strong, this spear helped me win my chiefdom. Now it waits for someone young and strong to win it back."

"Let me try it," said Ka-ui-lani eagerly. He lifted the heavy spear easily and aimed it at a distant tree.

"E . . . Ka-ui-lani! Not to the forest! Your enemy lies at sea!" said a high thin voice.

Ka-ui-lani turned to see why his father spoke in such a strange voice; turned to see his father smiling at his surprise.

"It is the Talking Spear," he explained. "To the one who wields it, this spear gives counsel."

"Maikai! Good!" said Ka-ui-lani. "Talking Spear, how shall we plan our campaign?"

"E . . . Ka-ui-lani," said the spear, "send men to the forest to cut down hau saplings and set them upright halfway across the mouth of the bay. Tomorrow I will tell you more."

So Ka-ui-lani sent men to the forest to cut down hau saplings and set them upright halfway across the mouth of the bay. On the morrow when he looked down, he saw that the saplings had grown and interwoven, forming a great, tangled thicket.

"What next, Talking Spear?" he asked.

"E . . . Ka-ui-lani," said the spear, "set men to carving life-sized images of wood and stand them in a line on the far shore of the bay."

So Ka-ui-lani set men to carving life-sized images of wood and stood them in a line on the far shore of the bay.

"What now, Talking Spear?" he asked.

"E . . . Ka-ui-lani," said the spear, "hide men with spears in the

thicket, then set a great fire to attract the enemy. Lead him into the bay where you and your men can attack. I will do the rest."

So Ka-ui-lani hid men with spears in the thicket and set a great fire to attract the enemy.

Akua-of-the-Swollen-Billows saw the smoke and said, "My old enemy is not dead, as I thought, but he soon will be!" and he came swimming to the foot of the pali and called up in a thundering voice, "E, Kea-hua! Come forth!"

A strong young figure appeared on top of the pali and a strong young voice replied:

"E, Akua-of-the-Swollen-Billows!
Come and meet Ka-ui-lani,
Son of High Chief Kea-hua,
Slayer of Akua!"

"Ho, my fine young cock!" retorted the sea kupua. "You, my slayer? Not so. You, my tasty meal!" and he opened his jaws until the lower one rested on the beach and the upper on the top of the pali.

Ka-ui-lani looked at the gaping jaws, then at his carefully laid trap in the bay far below, and called out, "Wait! This is no fair fight! You are but a thing of skin and bones. If I leap upon your back from this pali, I shall kill you with a single stroke. But I would not have it said that I killed you unfairly. Swim around to the bay and there we shall fight, both on the same level."

"Agreed," said Akua, licking his great lips. He turned about and swam toward the bay, and his going stirred up the sea like a great storm.

"Now!" cried the sea kupua. "Come forth and let me crunch your crisp bones!

Ka-ui-lani, armed with Talking Spear, appeared at the edge of the thicket. "Here I wait," he answered. "Come and take me!"

Akua swam into the bay and down to the end where Ka-ui-lani waited. He opened his great jaws to swallow him at a single gulp. But at Ka-ui-lani's signal, a swarm of spears came flying from the warriors hidden in the thicket. Each found its mark in the soft, tender coils of the sea kupua's body. He roared with pain, writhing and thrashing about in an effort to dislodge the spears. When he saw that he could not, he turned and swam frantically toward the opening of the bay, to escape.

But at Ka-ui-lani's second signal, the life-sized images came alive, came stalking down into the water, and closed off the sea kupua's escape. Then Ka-ui-lani, with one well-placed throw of his magic spear, put an end to Akua-of-the-Swollen-Billows.

High Chief Kea-hua made joyful preparations for returning home to rebuild his recovered chiefdom. But Ka-ui-lani noticed the sadness of his mother Kau-hao, and learned that she grieved for her daughter, taken to Oahu by the grandparents soon after her birth. All she knew of her was that a shimmering rainbow arched above her at her birth and followed her as she left.

"With the help of Talking Spear I shall find her, my mother, and bring her home for a visit," Ka-ui-lani promised, and set out for Oahu.

At sunset, he landed on a beach there, and Talking Spear said, "Follow this shore until you come to a lone wiliwili tree. There I will meet you." The spear flew on and soon was lost from sight.

Ka-ui-lani ran along the beach until he caught sight of the lone wiliwili tree but there was no sign of Talking Spear. He ran down to the water's edge and looked. No spear. Ran up and down the beach. No spear. Looked beneath the wiliwili tree, beside it, behind it. Nothing.

"E . . . Ka-ui-lani!" called a thin high voice. "Are you looking for me?" There, resting in the branches above his head, lay Talking Spear.

"You rascal spear! Come down!" cried Ka-ui-lani. "Any more tricks and I shall break you into firewood!"

"E . . . Ka-ui-lani," answered the spear in a laughing voice, "will firewood help you find your sister?"

"No," Ka-ui-lani admitted. "So no more jokes. Come down and tell me what to do."

The spear landed lightly in the sand at his feet. "Climb this tree," it said, "and look for a rainbow."

Ka-ui-lani climbed the tree. "I see no rainbow," he reported. "Only a red mist moving in from the sea."

"Look again," said the spear.

Ka-ui-lani looked again. "The mist is forming a rainbow," he reported.

"Look again," said the spear. "The maiden beneath it is your sister."

Ka-ui-lani looked again. "No more tricks!" he cried. "I see no maiden! Only a great white bird with gleaming feathers."

"Such weak eyes!" the spear complained. "Look again."

Ka-ui-lani looked again. Now the rainbow arched above the beach and beneath it was a maiden gathering sea moss. He climbed down and began to run. "She is there! I must speak to her!"

"Wait!" commanded Talking Spear. "You will frighten her off. Wait until she starts home, then follow her, keeping out of sight."

So Ka-ui-lani waited impatiently until the maiden started home, then followed her, keeping out of sight. Soon she came to a small grass house where an elderly woman was preparing the evening meal. Ka-ui-lani, hidden behind a sturdy coconut palm, saw the two eat, then prepare for the night. Through the open doorway, he saw the grandmother gather sleeping-kapa and, instead of spreading it for a bed, curl it up into a nest.

He glanced back at the maiden, but there was no maiden! Where she had sat, a sleek white tern now sat, preening her glossy feathers. As Ka-ui-lani stared, open-mouthed, the bird hopped into the house and settled down in the kapa nest with her head tucked beneath her wing.

"Your sister Bird Maiden is kupua," Talking Spear whispered. "You must wait until she is fast asleep, then seize her. No matter what she does, hold fast!"

Ka-ui-lani waited while the grandmother lay down, waited until dawn came and his muscles ached, then tiptoeing to the open doorway, he reached in and seized the sleeping bird. She woke with a frightened cry and Ka-ui-lani found that holding her was no easy task, for his kupua sister had supernatural strength. She managed to free her wings and fly up, and Ka-ui-lani holding fast to her feet, was carried with her. Up . . . up . . . up . . . she flew to dizzying heights. Ka-ui-lani, looking down at the tiny grass house below, wondered how long before he went crashing down upon it.

Then without warning, the white tern was gone. In its place was a fierce brown hawk that tore at his hands with its cruel beak.

"Wait, Bird Maiden! I am your brother!" Ka-ui-lani cried, but the wind snatched his words and carried them off.

He sensed another change and glancing up, saw the hawk turn into a formidable black albatross that beat at him with powerful wings.

Ka-ui-lani felt his arms grow numb and knew that he could not hold on much longer. The albatross dived and Ka-ui-lani saw the jagged line of rocks along the coast coming toward him at a terrifying speed. The albatross swooped inland over the small grass house. Ka-ui-lani closed his eyes, waiting to be dashed to the ground. Then from below came a thin high voice:

"E . . . Bird Maiden! Hold!
Would you kill your brother?
Your brother Ka-ui-lani?
Your brother with a message
From your mother on Kauai?"

The sickening dive ended. The albatross went gliding down to the beach and Ka-ui-lani found himself standing on the sand, facing a fair maiden, his sister, while overhead a rainbow shimmered.

The grandmother came running. There followed a joyful reunion: brother and sister, grandmother and grandson. There were eager questions about Ka-ui-lani's parents; cheering replies about the death of the sea kupua. There were admiring comments on the ingenuity of Talking Spear, and one tart comment from the spear itself. "Would you believe that this one threatened to break me up for firewood?"

"No more threats," Ka-ui-lani assured him heartily. "You have made up for all your tricks. But for you I should now be food for fish on this rocky coast. Come, it is time to take Bird Maiden home.

After Bird Maiden's happy reunion with her parents, Ka-ui-lani returned to Oahu for a time. He had not been there long when a message came. The King of Oahu wished to see him.

The king welcomed him warmly, offered food and drink, then said, "I have heard that you defeated the sea kupua and won back your father's chiefdom. Is this true?"

"It is true," Ka-ui-lani answered.

"Then you are the one I need," said the king, "for I am in grave danger of losing my kingdom."

"Who is your enemy?" Ka-ui-lani asked.

"Ha!" said the king bitterly. "My enemy is my friend, the King of Maui. He owns a kupua cock who wins every fight. Now my friend has challenged me. I want you to inspect my fighting birds and tell me their chances."

Ka-ui-lani had opened his mouth to say, "But I know nothing of fighting birds," when Talking Spear gave him such a poke in the ribs that he stopped short. "I shall be happy to give you an opinion," he heard himself saying.

"Good," said the king and went off to summon his keeper.

Talking Spear said crossly, "If the king wants an expert, be an expert!"

"But what do I know of fighting birds?" Ka-ui-lani protested.

"You have me!" retorted Talking Spear. "Point me at the cock in question. I will lean toward a winner, away from a loser."

Ka-ui-lani accompanied the king to the chicken house. The keeper brought out a dark red cock with a proud red comb.

"What do you think of him?" the king asked eagerly.

Ka-ui-lani tipped his head to one side and considered. "A handsome bird, this one," he said, pointing with his spear. The spear leaned away from the cock. "But he will not win against the kupua cock."

The king shrugged. "The next one!"

The keeper brought out a strong brown cock with gold-rimmed eyes. Ka-ui-lani tipped his head to the other side and considered. "A strong bird, this one," he said, pointing with his spear. Again the spear leaned away. "But not strong enough to defeat the kupua cock."

The king frowned. "My prize cock!" he ordered.

The keeper brought out a powerful bird with gleaming bronze body and tall green tail feathers. Ka-ui-lani tipped his head forward and considered. "Both handsome and powerful, this one," he said, pointing with his spear. The spear swerved away from this one too. "But I am sorry to say, even this one cannot defeat the kupua cock."

"Auwe!" cried the king. "What am I to do? I have no other fighting birds! The King of Maui will surely win my kingdom from me. Is there nothing you can do to help me?"

Ka-ui-lani raised the spear to his shoulder and it whispered in his ear, "Bird Maiden!"

"Perhaps I could borrow a bird for you," Ka-ui-lani suggested.

"A winner?" demanded the king.

"A winner," said Ka-ui-lani.

"Able to defeat the kupua cock?"

"Able to defeat the kupua cock. Arrange your match. I shall go and fetch the bird."

Soon Ka-ui-lani returned, but to the king's dismay, he came empty-handed. "You could not get the bird?" he asked.

"I could," said Ka-ui-lani.

"Then why did you not bring it?" demanded the king.

"I did," replied Ka-ui-lani.

"Where is it?"

"Here." Ka-ui-lani opened the folds of his shoulder cape and revealed an egg.

The king gasped. "You would let me wager my kingdom on a cock yet unborn?"

Ka-ui-lani nodded. "This is no ordinary bird," he assured the king. "I shall tend it in the keeper's house. Call when you need us."

The king shook his head dolefully and went to welcome his visitors. A crowd gathered. Soon over the babble of voices and the crowing of cocks sounded the arrogant voice of the Maui king. "Bring forth your first cock! I can use your royal feather cloak, my friend."

"And I, yours," answered the King of Oahu weakly. He nodded and his keeper brought out the dark red cock.

"Bid him farewell," said the King of Maui. "He has not long to live." He uncovered his kupua cock. It was glossy and black as lava, with tall curling tail feathers. He set it on the ground and it shook itself, swelling to twice its former size.

The two birds were placed in the ring. They eyed each other warily. Swiftly the kupua cock leaped upon its adversary. There was a beating of wings, a single terrified squawk, and the dark red cock lay dead.

Silently the King of Oahu took off his royal feather cloak and handed it to the King of Maui. Grinning, the man put it on, strutting back and forth before an admiring crowd.

"If your next cock is no better," he said insolently, "you may give me your royal canoe now and save your miserable bird."

The King of Oahu flushed angrily. "We will fight," he said coldly. "My royal canoe against yours."

The keeper brought out the brown cock to face the black. This time, the brown bird leaped to the attack, but before it could land a second blow, the kupua cock struck him dead.

The King of Oahu gestured and his servant handed over the steering paddle to the royal canoe.

"Enough of playing games," said the King of Maui. "Put up your third cock. The stake—half your kingdom!"

A groan went up from the Oahu men, a cheer from the Maui visitors. The keeper brought out the prize bronze cock. It eyed the kupua cock belligerently, ruffled its gleaming bronze feathers, and struck with its sharp claws. There was a wild flurry of tearing claws, beating wings, and flying feathers. When it was over, the kupua cock was wounded, but the bronze cock lay dead.

The King of Maui swept up his wounded bird and turned to leave. "When you have had time to acquire more losers, let me know," he said, "and I shall return for the other half of your kingdom."

"Hold!" cried the King of Oahu. "I challenge you to one more fight!"

The Maui king's eyes gleamed angrily at having someone else take the center of attention. "Bring out your fourth loser," he said scornfully.

The keeper summoned Ka-ui-lani. He appeared with a beautiful snow-white bird in his arms. A murmur of admiration swept the crowd. He set the bird on the ground. There was a startled silence then a ripple of laughter that grew and spread. "A hen! The King of Maui's cock challenged by a hen!"

This turn of affairs was not at all to the Maui king's liking. His eyes narrowed.

"One final match," he conceded. "The stakes—your bones!"

The King of Oahu paled. "Why not the remaining half of my kingdom?" he suggested.

The King of Maui grinned—a cruel grin. "When I win your bones will I not take the remainder of your kingdom anyway?" he asked. "Your bones! Bet or withdraw!"

There was no withdrawing with honor. "My bones against yours," said the King of Oahu. With a despairing glance at Ka-ui-lani, he set the white hen in the ring. She looked pitifully small and frail as she faced the fierce black cock.

The cock leaped to the attack. Feathers flew. Dust flew. There was an angry squawk from the cock but no outcry from the hen. When the dust settled, the cock had lost his proud look and dragged one wing. The hen was no longer white but spotted; spotted with her own blood.

Another attack. Another flurry. The two drew apart. Now the cock had a deep cut above one eye and crouched, gasping for breath. The hen's feathers were more red than white.

Angrily the King of Maui urged his cock on, but it huddled at the edge of the ring, trembling. The white hen ruffled her feathers. She seemed to grow larger and larger until, facing the cock stood a fierce brown chicken hawk with powerful spreading wings.

The cock gave a startled squawk, flew gabbling from the ring, and dived behind the Maui king for shelter.

Roars of laughter swept the crowd. "The champion cock defeated by a hen! Who has ever seen the like of it?"

Scowling, the Maui king snatched up his shivering cock and started off.

"Wait!" cried a stern voice.

The King of Maui turned to find Ka-ui-lani with his spear aimed at his throat. He gulped.

"Did you not wager your bones? And lose?" Ka-ui-lani demanded. "It is time to settle your account."

Gone was the king's arrogance. He was as sorry a sight now as his defeated cock, as both stood waiting for death.

"Hold!" said the King of Oahu. "What need have I for your bones? Return my cloak, my canoe, my land, and go. Do not return."

The King of Maui's servant drew off the royal feather cloak and returned it, picked up the royal steering paddle and returned it, took the shivering kupua cock and carried it to the waiting canoe. The miserable figure of the Maui king followed after.

The crowd drifted away, and the King of Oahu turned to thank Ka-ui-lani, who knelt at the ringside. Gone now was the fierce brown chicken hawk, if indeed there had ever been one. In its place huddled a small, weary, blood-spattered white hen. Tenderly Ka-ui-lani took her in his arms and stroked her.

"Is she badly hurt?" the king asked.

"With rest and care she will recover," Ka-ui-lani replied.

"I will see that she has the very best of care," said the king.

"She is braver than any fighting cock I have ever owned, and I must have her! Ask any price you wish!"

Ka-ui-lani stared, speechless. "I cannot sell her," he murmured at last.

"Any price!" the king repeated firmly.

There came a sudden clatter. Ka-ui-lani's spear, resting against the keeper's house, fell noisily to the ground. The king turned for a moment, at the sound. When he looked back, Ka-ui-lani's arms were empty, and in the sky above him a snow-white tern was winging its way homeward.

Soon Ka-ui-lani was on his way too, his trusty spear across his shoulder.

"E . . . Ka-ui-lani," said the familiar high thin voice. "Where is the one who spoke of breaking me up for firewood?"

"Gone," Ka-ui-lani answered. "Gone forever. Soon you will be back in your place of honor in my father's spear rack. Then all his people will hear how first his chiefdom, then his son, and last his daughter, were saved by the wisdom of Talking Spear."

The spear gave a satisfied chuckle, and Ka-ui-lani went on his way, whistling.

Opele-of-the-Long-Sleeps

IT WAS THE MOON of Ikuwa, the month of the loud voice, with noise from above and noise from below. Thunder rumbled through the skies, surf crashed upon the shore, and heralds went about the district calling loudly for all to bring their tax offerings to the chief.

Opele, hearing the summons, smiled, for he was a good farmer and his crops were ready for harvest: plump sweet potatoes, fine wet-land kalo, smooth-skinned gourds.

A good farmer? The finest in Waipio, said his neighbors but they looked on him with awe, not envy. Truly, the gods have given him a special power over growing things, they thought, but at what a price! These spells that come upon him—they come when he is happiest—and who knows where his spirit wanders while his body sleeps? Suppose one day his spirit loses its way and fails to return!

But such thoughts did not bother Opele. His mind was on more

43

cheerful matters as he began his harvest. Today he would gather his offering, then freshly bathed and wearing his best malo, would attend opening ceremonies of the Makahiki festival and with other farmers and fishermen, present his tax offerings to the chief. Then there would be feasting and dancing and great tournaments of sports. He would surely see Malia there, and if his crops were judged best in the district, as they might well be, perhaps find courage to ask her to be his wife.

His harvesting was half-finished when the great drowsiness came upon him. Dropping his digging stick, he stretched out beside the stream to rest. Soon he was fast asleep.

The Makahiki festival opened. The farmers and fishermen presented their tax offerings to the chief. The feasting and dancing and tournaments began. But Opele still slept by the stream bank. Malia, seeing him nowhere about, smiled upon his rival.

On and on Opele slept, into the drenching time. Heavy rains, swelling the stream to overflowing, carried him off. He woke to the sound of rumbling thunder, woke to find himself far from home, on the banks of a fast-flowing stream. He saw a young woman coming to the stream to fill her water gourd. Opele got to his feet and spoke softly, so as not to frighten her.

"I am called Opele. What place is this? Can you tell me where I may find food?"

"This is Waimanu," the young woman answered. "I am called Kaeko and the house of my father has food for a stranger. Come."

Opele met Kaeko's father and spent some time with him. He helped plant his crops, tend his earth oven, catch his fish. Then, having found a warm home among strangers, he asked for Kaeko as his wife. Her father gave his consent and the two were married.

Those were happy days for Opele. Now he had a wife for whom to light the fires and fill the earth oven. He built her a fine grass house not far from her father's home. He rose early to catch

her favorite fish. He worked late to raise her favorite crops. Only one small worry nibbled at his mind. He knew that he should tell Kaeko of his trances but he put off the telling. Why worry her? Was he not sleeping a single night at a time now? Perhaps his sleeping spells had come to an end.

When Kaeko gave him the glad news that a child was expected, Opele knew he could put off his telling no longer. He told her of the deep sleeps that sometimes came upon him. He calmed her fears and assured her that he would wake at the sound of some great noise. Then, the telling over, his mind returned to her joyful news.

A son! They must have a son! Opele took two hinalea fish, wrapped them in ki leaves, and broiled them over the coals. Then, kneeling before the family shrine, he prayed:

"O Lono, god of growing things,
Accept this offering.
The first fish is for you.
Kaeko will eat the second.
O Lono, hear my prayer:
Grant us a son.
A son to till the field,
A son to raise the kalo,
A son to atone for his father's failures.
My prayer is ended."

The months slipped by and when the moon of Ikuwa came again, Opele's prayer was answered. Kaeko delivered a sturdy son whom they named Kalele. At his squalls, Opele exclaimed, "Hear this noisy one! He could be the chief's herald! He speaks with a voice like thunder!"

That night, Opele offered a prayer of thanksgiving to his god Lono, then lay down to dream of his infant son already grown, working beside him in the kalo patch.

Morning came. Kalele woke, demanding to be fed. Kaeko, rising to hush the baby's crying, looked anxiously at Opele, still sleeping soundly.

Kalele squalled louder. Opele stirred; stirred and woke with a rueful grin. "No need to worry about long sleeps with this one about!" he said.

Kaeko nodded, smiling. With a small sigh of relief she carried the baby out into the morning sunlight.

Soon Opele came out, bearing a closely-twined basket. "This day calls for celebration," he said. "I am going down to the rocks to gather sea moss and opihi while the tide is low."

Kaeko smoothed the infant's hair. "When this small noisy one is older, I shall tell him how his father the farmer, braved the sea waters to gather delicacies to celebrate his birth. Be careful when the tide turns, my husband."

Opele laughed. "I shall be back with a full basket long before the tide turns."

Kaeko watched him stride down the trail to the beach, then busied herself with the baby's feeding and bathing. She had put the child on his sleeping kapa for a nap, and had gathered up his small wrappings to wash in the stream when she heard hurrying footsteps on the trail. She ran out to meet her husband.

It was not her husband she met but a neighboring fisherman with news of Opele—sad news. One of his spells had come upon him as he clambered over the sea-washed rocks. He had fallen into the water and been swept out to sea.

Over the sound of the turning tide rose the voice of Kaeko, mourning for Opele.

Opele, still sleeping, was washed upon the distant shore of Maui. He woke to the sound of crashing surf; woke to find himself on a lonely beach where a solitary fisherman stood in the distance, casting his net.

Opele made his way to him. "I am Opele, farmer of Waimanu. Can you help me find my way home?"

The fisherman shook his head. "No Waimanu on this island." He turned back to his casting.

Opele stumbled along the beach. To each person he met he cried, "I am Opele, farmer of Waimanu . . . husband of Kaeko . . . father of a newborn son, Kalele. Can you help me find them?"

They looked on him, some with pity, some with impatience, but their answers were always the same. "No Waimanu on this island, and we have been on no other island."

Opele found a cave for shelter. What use to build a house with no wife to live in it, no infant son to fill it with his stormy cries? Kind-hearted neighbors gave him a few food plants and he raised enough to repay them and keep himself from starvation. Sadly he lived through the empty days, the lonely nights, and now, with happiness gone from his life, he suffered no more sleeping spells.

The years crawled by. Four . . . eight . . . twelve of them. Whenever the moon laid a silver pathway upon the water, Opele dreamed of following that pathway back to his home, back to Kaeko, back to Kalele. How tall would his son be now, with twelve years behind him? Had Kaeko taught him to use his father's digging stick? Was he a good son? A fine farmer? Or just another sleeper?

Opele had little contact with his neighbors, none at all with their children, for sight of them only added to his sorrow. When a boy came whistling by the kalo patch where he was setting out young plants, Opele frowned and did not speak.

The boy carried a smooth stick balanced across his shoulders and he tilted it, first one way then the other, peering at Opele's work.

"Your kalo lines are crooked," he commented.

Scowling, Opele checked his lines and moved one plant slightly to the left.

"Still crooked."

Opele turned angrily. "My kalo patches were the best in the district, long before you were born!" he declared. "How is it that now my lines are crooked?"

The boy grinned. "Perhaps you need a better digging stick." He held out the one he carried.

Opele stared. That was his own stick, his favorite, the one he had made to till his first field for Kaeko. He recognized the knot in the handle, remembered the day he had shaped the flat blade.

"That is my own!" he said.

"And I am your own," said the boy. "Kalele. Your son and Kaeko's."

Opele shook his head in wonder. "How many times I have seen you in my dreams—and now you are here! Tell me of Kaeko! Is she well?"

"She is, and still waits for your return."

"I have never known for certain, what happened on that sad day," Opele lamented.

"My mother has told me the story many times over," said Kalele, "how you went to gather sea moss and opihi to celebrate my birth; how one of your sleeping spells came upon you and you fell from the rocks and were swept out to sea."

"I thought it might be so," Opele answered. "But you—how did you get here?"

"My mother planned that one day I should set out and find you. She taught me that bold wishing and brave action can accomplish much—and as you see, she was right."

"How did it come about?" Opele asked.

Kalele's eyes danced. "First, I wished boldly to find you. Then, when I met some fishermen setting out for this island, I acted bravely and asked for a place in their canoe."

Opele smiled in spite of himself. "And has your bold wishing and brave action provided a way home for us?" he asked.

"It has," said Kalele. "The fishermen know I am searching for you. They are holding a place for two on their return trip."

Opele laughed, his first laugh in many long years, and the sound was good to hear. "So my son the squaller has become a bold wisher!" he said. "Come. Bathe, eat, and rest. In the morning we shall hold your fishermen to their offer."

The lonely cave echoed that night with the sound of man-talk, father-and-son talk, and it was late before Opele and Kalele lay down to sleep.

When the morning star glowed in the sky, Kalele woke. But Opele slept on; slept heavily, then woke with a start to the sound of a great voice shouting:

"Opele-of-the-Long-Sleeps!
It is time to awake!
The fishermen are waiting;
Your son Kalele is waiting;
Your wife Kaeko is waiting;
It is time to journey home."

Opele sat up, blinking. Aia la! This son of his had a voice like thunder, indeed! Perhaps one day he would be herald to a chief. Meantime, if the joy of returning home should bring on another of Opele's long sleeps, there was Kalele-of-the-Loud-Voice to waken him.

Smiling, he shouldered his digging stick. Side by side, father and son started down to the beach where a canoe waited.

Kalele the Bold Wisher

KALELE, grown to manhood, had little of his father Opele's gift for growing things. True, the gods had given him his own special gift—he was a swift and tireless runner—but that was small comfort in the time of famine that now plagued the land. In his small house on the hillside, Kalele and his friend Keino-the-Timid went hungry to bed. To forget their hunger they passed the time in wishing.

Keino spoke above the rumble of his empty stomach. "My wish is that tomorrow we catch a fat eel, cook it in banana leaves, and eat our fill."

Kalele grinned. "My wish is that tomorrow we be invited by the high chief to his royal eating house, feast upon baked pig from the royal pigpens and fat milk-fish from the royal fishponds, drink awa from the royal cups, served by the chief himself. . . ."

"Stop!" Keino squealed.

"But I have not finished," said Kalele. "After we have eaten and drunk our fill, the chief will bring forth his two lovely daughters to be our wives. That is my wish."

"Auwe!" cried Keino, trembling. "If anyone should overhear your rash talk it would mean our death!"

"Nonsense!" Kalele answered. "Hear what my mother taught me: bold wishing and brave action can accomplish much!"

But Keino would play the game no longer. He turned his face to the wall and spoke no more.

In the morning, Kalele wakened to the sound of Keino's frightened cry. He found him outside, staring in terror at a polished bone dagger plunged into the ground beside their doorsill.

"Look! A royal dagger! Someone from the chief's household overheard your rash talk! It means death for us!"

Kalele shrugged. "Death comes for each of us at some time but there is no need to run to meet it."

Keino pointed toward the royal grounds below. "No need to run to meet it!" he repeated in a terrified whisper. "The chief's men bring it to our door!"

Up the hillside came a company of the chief's men, armed with sharp stone axes. Kalele watched them, unmoved. "If death comes, it comes," he said. "But if it passes by, there is tomorrow."

The two waited silently as the chief's men drew nearer, reached them, and passed by without a glance. Soon from the forest beyond came the sound of chopping.

Kalele laughed. "They came seeking wood, not blockheads."

Next morning when the two looked down on the royal grounds, they saw two new dwellings, and coming up the hillside, a procession of the chief's warriors—four carrying spears, four the royal litter.

Keino trembled. "Surely death comes up the hillside for us today, with a litter to carry back our dead bodies!"

"How many commoners ride to death in a chief's litter?" Kalele asked. "Be grateful that we make such an impressive exit."

A warrior strode up to them. "We have orders to bring you both to the chief," he said. "Come!" He pointed to the litter.

Kalele picked up his club and took his place in the litter. Keino crept in beside him. The procession made its way down the hillside.

The chief himself welcomed them to the royal eating house. They feasted on baked pig from the royal pigpens and fat milkfish from the royal fishponds, drank awa from the royal cups, served by the chief himself.

Kalele ate with good appetite, enjoying the fine food and drink. Keino ate but a few mouthfuls and drank not at all. "Everything is just as you said!" he whispered. "The chief plays a grim joke on us before having us killed!"

"Wait and see," said Kalele.

When the meal was over, the chief said, "Let us go to the long house. We have matters to discuss." He rose and led the way. There, his two lovely daughters joined them, one beside Kalele, one beside Keino. Kalele smiled. Keino grew pale.

The chief studied the two men thoughtfully, then spoke. "I am told that one of you is a bold wisher," he said.

"P-p-please, O Chief! It was but a joke," Keino stammered.

"A joke?" the chief repeated softly. "I hope not. It is the reason for your being here. My enemy, Chief Pueo the Owl, seeks my land. I need a bold man to defeat him. Who better than the one who made such a bold wish?"

"We are yours to command, O Chief," said Kalele.

"Good," said the chief. "I have had built a dwelling for each of you on the royal grounds. Each may wed one of my daughters and live there until needed. When Chief Pueo is about to strike, I shall call you. You had best be ready with a good plan to defeat him. It would be unfortunate to have my daughters made wives and widows within a moon, eh?"

As the chief ordered, so it was done. For Kalele, the days were filled with joy; for Keino, with fear and foreboding. Then came the day Keino had been dreading . . . Chief Pueo was preparing to attack.

"What shall we do?" Keino pleaded. "It is time for the battle!"

Kalele shook his head. "What man with a beautiful new bride feels like going to battle?"

"But one of us must go or the chief will have us both killed!" Keino cried. "I am no warrior but if you will not go, I must!"

So Keino reported to the chief and was put in charge of his royal forces. He led them forward until the enemy could be seen in the distance and then, for want of a better plan, brought them to a halt. To his captain he said, "Lead the men forward. I will slip around behind and surprise the enemy from the rear."

When Keino-the-Timid reached the battlefield, he found the battle over. Many lay slain, among them a chief—the image of his god still standing beside him, the circle of his spearsmen still about him, but his feather helmet and cape gone. His captain arriving with his men congratulated Keino on his strategy. Keino, bewildered, said nothing.

The chief was greatly pleased at this victory and Keino-the-Timid gained a reputation for great military skill, and rare modesty.

The old moon died and the new moon was born. Word came that Pueo had rallied his remaining forces and was about to make another attack.

Keino-the-Timid, remembering the success of his original plan, repeated it. Again he found the battle over, many of the enemy slain, and among them another chief stripped of feather helmet and cape. He turned, puzzled, to his approaching captain.

"Another victory!" cried the captain. "And this time I saw the rascal who has been carrying off the feather garments! He ran swiftly into the woods on our side of the battlefield."

Keino nodded gravely and said nothing. What could he say?

A third attack came and Keino-the-Timid used his plan a third time, arriving to find Chief Pueo himself slain and stripped of his feather garments, his remaining forces wiped out. At the edge of the field he spied a fleeing figure.

"There!" he shouted. His captain hurled his spear. They saw the spear strike, saw the runner pluck it from his shoulder, and run off.

The high chief's forces returned home, the men triumphant, their leader confused, their captain suspicious. The chief, over-joyed at Pueo's defeat, proclaimed a great feast. "This Keino-the-Timid is poorly named," he said jovially. "We must find a more suitable name for him."

"O Chief, before you do that, may I speak?" the captain asked. The chief nodded. The captain said, "I do not believe Keino was responsible for our success. Twice I saw a mysterious runner flee-ing the battlefield, carrying the feather garments of slain chiefs. I believe it was he who defeated the enemy, not Keino-the-Timid!"

The chief frowned. "Who is this man?"

"He is the man with a fresh spear-wound in his right shoulder," the captain answered.

The chief ordered all his men to pass before him but found no man with such a wound. "What now?" he asked.

The captain spoke again. "Is this every able-bodied man, O Chief?"

"All but my lazy son-in-law Kalele, who spends his time eating and sleeping."

"May I summon him?" the captain persisted. The chief nodded and the captain went off.

Soon he returned. Behind him came Kalele, swift-running Kalele, wearing the rich feather helmet and cape of Chief Pueo the Owl. Behind him walked his wife, bearing the capes and helmets of two other chiefs.

The captain drew back the cape from Kalele's right shoulder and pointed to the spear wound. "This is the man who brought us victory!" he declared.

The chief welcomed Kalele and with great ceremony transferred the royal forces to his charge. Then in anger he turned and shouted, "Where is that pretender, Keino-the-Timid?"

Keino was brought to stand trembling before the chief.

Kalele broke in. "O Chief, if we are to maintain a victorious army, there is one thing I must have."

"Name it," said the chief.

"The right man as my advisor," Kalele replied.

"Any man in my chiefdom. Name him."

"Keino-the-Timid," said Kalele.

The high chief looked astounded, the captain scornful, and Keino, poor Keino, bewildered.

"Why me?" he asked.

Kalele laughed. "Who else? My friend, with you at my side, death will never catch me unaware, for I shall have Keino-the-Timid to warn me of his coming."

The Champion Spearsman

FROM THE TIME of his youth, Kapunohu had wanted but one thing—a perfect spear. He tested every spear he saw. He had spears made for him by the finest spearmakers in the district. He learned the art of spearmaking and made his own. But never could he find a perfect spear. Each one left something to be desired.

Then one day as he made his way to the playing field, a spear flew past him with a sound like the rushing wind, and came to rest far ahead of him. Eager to examine it, Kapunohu ran and picked it up. He rubbed the gleaming wood and found the finish perfect. He tested the blade and found its cutting edge perfect. He balanced the shaft and found its balance perfect. Then he drew back his arm and sent the spear flying.

It skimmed through the air, pierced a young palm tree, sailed through it, and came to rest at a greater distance than Kapunohu had ever thrown before. Here was the perfect spear at last! Here was the spear he must have!

Kapunohu turned to see who owned the spear. There, coming toward him, was an angry man with pale, staring eyes. He held out his hand. "My spear!"

"Hold," Kapunohu answered. "I have never seen such a spear. I will trade you four fine spears for this one."

"No," said the stranger.

"Ten!"

"No," said the stranger.

"What do you ask for it?"

"I will not part with it," came the stranger's reply.

"But I must have it!" Kapunohu pleaded. "All my life I have searched for a perfect spear and now, at last, I have found one! Reconsider, please!"

"No!"

"A wager!" cried Kapunohu. "Take the spear from me and it is yours again; fail and it becomes mine!"

This time, the stranger made no answer, just came toward him. As he came, Kapunohu saw something that chilled his blood. The man left no footprints. This was no human! This was a spirit! Yet he would battle even a spirit to possess such a perfect spear.

The spirit came on. Kapunohu dodged, feinted. The spirit grabbed him. Kapunohu squirmed free. On and on went the struggle but Kapunohu managed to hold onto the spear. Then suddenly, the spirit stood still, fixed him with his pale, staring eyes, and murmured something.

Kapunohu found himself frozen to the spot, hands glued to the shaft.

"A truce!" Kapunohu cried. "You will not give up the spear; I cannot. Let us work together. What can you do alone with this perfect spear? As soon as men recognize you as a spirit, they will flee. You will never find a competitor worthy of your spear. Be my aumakua! With you as my god, there is nothing we cannot do with such a spear!"

The pale, staring eyes did not warm but they lost a little of their coldness. This Kapunohu had courage, no doubt of that. Had he the skill to match? If he had, this arrangement he suggested could be amusing. "Agreed," said the spirit, releasing his spell.

Kapunohu moved again but eyed him with suspicion. "Truly?"

"Truly."

So began a strange partnership . . . Kapunohu, Kani-kaa, and Rushing Wind . . . man, spirit, and perfect spear. Since Kani-kaa remained invisible a good part of the time, Kapunohu soon gained an outstanding reputation for his spearsmanship.

Now that Kapunohu had found his perfect spear, and a spirit aumakua as well, he was eager for contest. Kapunohu lived at this time with his sister and brother-in-law, Kukui-pahu, Chief of Kohala. The chief, jealous of Kapunohu's new-found fame, sought a way to put the young spearsman in his place.

One morning as he sat with his followers in the men's eating house, he saw his chance. When Kapunohu stopped to wash his hands in the calabash at the door, his brother-in-law called out, "E Kapunohu! When you have washed, where do you plan to eat?"

"With you," Kapunohu replied, puzzled.

"Oh?" said Kukui-pahu. "I did not invite you. Did someone here perhaps invite Kapunohu?"

"No," answered Kukui-pahu's men in chorus.

Kapunohu, who had thought to offer himself and his spear in his brother-in-law's service turned away without eating and left the home of Kukui-pahu. Now the chief's land was bordered on one side by a row of wiliwili trees that stretched as far as the eye

could see. There were said to be eight hundred trees in the row. Overcome with fury at Kukui-pahu's unprovoked treatment, Kapunohu hurled his spear, Rushing Wind, at the first tree. It sailed cleanly through and continued out of sight. When he reached the far end of the line he found it waiting for him. It had cut through the eight hundred wiliwili trees at a single thrust.

Kapunohu continued on his way until he came to the section of the Kohala district under Chief Niu-lii. He knew that his brother-in-law controlled the greater part of the Kohala district and Chief Niu-lii the remainder. The two chiefs were constantly at war. Kapunohu, seeing a way to repay Kukui-pahu's insult, offered his services to Chief Niu-lii, who accepted them gladly.

When Kukui-pahu attacked again, Kapunohu led Niu-lii's forces against him. It was a fierce battle. Spears flew back and forth so fast that the sound was like a great windstorm, and the dust that arose like a great thundercloud. When the dust settled, three thousand of Kukui-pahu's men lay slain, and among them, Kukui-pahu, with Kapunohu's spear in his heart.

But a remnant of Kukui-pahu's army remained, led by the great warrior, Pa-o-pele. When Niu-lii's men heard this, they begged Kapunohu not to pursue him.

"No one can win against this one!" they cried. "He carries a war club like no other! When he holds it up, its tip is wet with the mists of heaven. When he lays it down, it reaches from mountain to sea. It is said that four thousand men would be needed to carry it! What chance have we against such a foe?"

"I will go out against him alone," Kapunohu declared. Carrying his spear, Rushing Wind, he went forth. But when Pa-o-pele appeared, Kapunohu's blood ran cold, for the man was tremendous and his voice like the roar of thunder.

Kapunohu called on his spirit 'aumakua and Kani-kaa answered.

"Do not fear this thunderer. He is all noise, no strength. When I leap upon his back and bite him, hurl your spear and kill him."

Kapunohu nodded but through his mind ran a chilling thought. Would the spirit truly help him or was he planning revenge on Kapunohu for taking his spear? There was but one way to find out. Kapunohu went forward.

Huge rumbles of mirth shook Pa-o-pele when he saw Kapunohu. "Ho, Little One!" he cried. "Run, before my club crushes you! Run, while there is yet time!"

"Fight!" said Kapunohu.

Before Pa-o-pele could raise his great club, something fastened on his back and bit him. With a roar he tried to seize it. Then Kapunohu threw his spear. It hit Pa-o-pele squarely and passed on through, killing him instantly.

So the whole of Kohala came under the charge of Chief Niu-lii. So Kukui-pahu's insult was avenged. So Kapunohu and his aumakua, Kani-kaa, became closer companions than before.

High Chief Niu-lii would gladly have kept the young spearsman as commander of his forces, but Kapunohu was eager to be off. Calling upon his invisible aumakua, Kani-kaa, he set out for the beautiful island of Kauai in the western sea.

At Koloa, a friendly man offered to share his evening meal and lodging with him. But in the morning when he heard of Kapunohu's plan to circle the island, he begged him not to go on. "The great warrior Kemamo lives beyond here, with his wife, Wai-a-le-a-le. He allows no one to pass that way."

"Is he such an expert?" Kapunohu asked.

"He is."

"With what weapon? Spear? Club?"

"With slingshot."

"Ka!" said Kapunohu scornfully. "That is a plaything, not a weapon!"

"Not as Kemamo uses it," said the man. "He can throw a stone five miles with it and have it roll another mile after landing!"

"That I would see," said Kapunohu, and thanking the man for his hospitality, went on his way. His remarks flew ahead of him.

Soon he came face to face with Kemamo, barring the way.

"Your name?"

"Kapunohu from Kohala."

Kemamo glared. "The one who casts insults at my skill with the slingshot!"

"Not insults," Kapunohu answered, "the truth. Where I grew up, the slingshot is a plaything of small boys."

"Perhaps you would compete with me and my plaything," Kemamo suggested, "and lay a wager on the outcome."

"Gladly."

"What will you wager?"

"What thing of value does any traveler carry with him, other than his life? I will wager my life against yours," said Kapunohu.

"Agreed," said Kemamo. He led Kapunohu up to a hilltop and pointed. Far off in the hazy distance lay the village of Moloaa on the opposite side of the island. "The course will be from here to Moloaa. He who throws the greatest distance will be declared winner."

"Agreed," replied Kapunohu. "Your sling against my spear. The native son may go first."

Kemamo put a stone in his sling, whirled it about his head, and cast it from him. Through the valley, across the plain, into a coconut grove and out again went the stone. Over the ridge at Anahola it flew, a total distance of six miles. There it fell to the ground and rolled another mile, then came to rest.

"Let me see you do better!" cried Kemamo gleefully.

"Easily," said Kapunohu. Whispering a prayer to his invisible aumakua, Kapunohu hurled his spear.

Through the valley, across the plain, into the coconut grove and out again went the spear. But as it neared the ridge at Anahola, Kapunohu saw trouble ahead. The spear was flying too low to clear the ridge. If it struck and fell there, the contest was over, and his life, as well.

"Kani-kaa!" he whispered. "What shall I do?"

"Have faith," came the whispered reply.

Kapunohu held his breath. He saw the spear strike the mountain and pierce the ridge, leaving a hole behind it that can be seen to this day. On went the spear, to Moloaa and past. To Hanalei and past. To a beach ten miles beyond the spot where Kemamo's stone had fallen. There it fell, then rose, circled back, and put an end to the troublesome slingshot champion.

Today, on the island of Kauai, two mountains still stand. One, resembling a fallen warrior, is Kemamo; the other, known as the wettest spot on earth, is Wai-a-le-a-le, endlessly weeping for her slain husband.

Kapunohu returned to his friend at Koloa with the good news that now the way around the island was open. Then, with his aumakua, Kani-kaa, and his spear, Rushing Wind, he returned home to Kohala, for he had accomplished what he had set out to do.

So ended the strange partnership of Kapunohu, Kani-kaa, and Rushing Wind . . . man, spirit, and perfect spear.

The Boaster No Man Could Kill

KALAE-PUNI WAS A BOASTER from the very beginning. As a boy, he boasted that he would whip every boy of his age. He did. As a youth, he boasted that he would defeat every chief in his district. He did.

Now when such a boaster fails to carry out his boasts, he affords amusement, but when he unfailingly makes good these boasts, he is feared and plotted against.

Kalae-puni knew of the reputation he was gaining, and cultivated it. He let his hair grow long and shaggy as a bunch of olona fiber so people would say, "Here comes that wild man, Kalae-puni!" He joined in every shark hunt, plunging in and killing sharks with his bare hands, then saying, "Here are your sharks from the strong hands of Kalae-puni!"

When Kalae-puni began boasting that he would soon become high chief of Hawaii, there were angry mutterings among the people. "What of our ruling High Chief Keawe-nui?" they asked. "Do you plan to kill him?"

66

"No need for that," Kalae-puni retorted. "Already he is blink-eyed with age. Soon he will sleep summers and winters in death. When Kalae-puni is ready to rule, Keawe-nui will be gone."

When this latest boast reached the ears of the High Chief, Keawe-nui gathered about him his advisor Mokupane, those chiefs who were loyal to him (and these were many), and those who feared Kalae-puni (and these were more).

"It is time for this blink-eyed one to make way for Kalae-puni," the high chief announced.

His followers stared in consternation. "You would give up your chiefdom to this boaster?"

Keawe-nui smiled. "Temporarily," he answered. "Now tell me, if Kalae-puni were high chief and sharks threatened our people, how would he handle the matter?"

"That one?" said Mokupane. "He would plunge in and kill the sharks with his bare hands!"

"Excellent!" said Keawe-nui. "Now tell me this. In which waters are schools of sharks most often sighted?"

"The waters off the coast of Kohala," said a chief.

Keawe-nui nodded gravely. "I have heard that a swift and treacherous current flows from these waters past the deserted island of Kahoolawe. If a number of men were willing to go to that island and make certain preparations, I think we might see the end of our boaster."

The high chief soon had his volunteers. He outlined his plan to them and finished by saying, "Now it is time to spread the sad news of the passing of High Chief Keawe-nui."

As it was planned, so it was done. Before long, Kalae-puni appeared at the high chief's dwelling. "I have heard about Keawe-nui. . . ." he began.

"Auwe! So sad!" said Mokupane. "Our High Chief Keawe-nui is gone from us."

"It is as I expected," said Kalae-puni. "Now a new ruling chief is needed, and who is better qualified than Kalae-puni?"

"You are the very man we hoped for," Mokupane answered smoothly. "But do you not fear some jealous chief may try to kill you?"

"No man will ever kill Kalae-puni!" came the boastful reply.

So Kalae-puni took over as high chief of Hawaii and, for a few days, all was quiet. Then a delegation requested audience with the new high chief, and this, Kalae-puni graciously granted.

"O Chief," said the spokesman, "A great school of sharks threatens swimmer and fisherman in the waters off Kohala! What shall we do?"

"No problem," replied Kalae-puni. "I shall take care of the matter personally."

He set out at once for Kohala. Arriving there, he bowed to the watching crowds, then plunged into the water and began fighting sharks with his bare hands, killing a goodly number.

So busy was he in demonstrating his strength and courage that he failed to notice that he was drifting farther and farther from land. Before long, he found the current too strong to fight his way back.

For three days and three nights, Kalae-puni drifted, landing at last on the shore of the deserted island of Kahoolawe. Exhausted and suffering greatly from hunger and thirst, he struggled to his feet and stumbled along the beach towards a single lone shack in the distance.

An elderly couple came out to greet him. "Where do you come from?" they asked.

"From Kohala," Kalae-puni answered. "Fighting sharks, I was carried off by the current."

The old man and woman looked at the sea-soaked malo and the

long matted hair like a bunch of olona fiber. This is the one, they thought.

"I have been three days and nights in the sea," said Kalae-puni. "I need food. What do you have?"

"Only this," said the old woman. She handed him a calabash of dried fish.

Kalae-puni wolfed it down. "More!" he cried.

The old man pointed to the rack of fish drying in the sun. Kalae-puni gobbled those. Then he said, "I have a great thirst. Give me water."

"Auwe!" cried the old woman. "Only when it rains do we have fresh water. There has been no rain for weeks. We have a deep well but one must climb down into it to reach the water and we are too feeble for that."

"Show me this well. I am not too feeble!" Kalae-puni boasted.

The couple led him to the well. It was deep indeed, and around its rim stood a great pile of rocks.

"It is too deep for you," the old woman muttered, shaking her head.

"Nothing is too deep for Kalae-puni!" he boasted, and climbed down.

The old woman looked at the old man. "Now it is time," she said.

Fearfully the old man began rolling rocks down upon Kalae-puni.

But Kalae-puni, with his fierce strength, managed to free himself and began climbing up the wall of the well. "You treacherous old man!" he cried. "When I get up there I will make an end of you! No man will ever kill Kalae-puni!"

The old man, terrified, retreated. "We must run and hide!" he cried to his wife.

"Where would we hide from this one?" she asked scornfully. She walked to the mouth of the well, chose the biggest rock from the pile, and pushed it down on top of Kalae-puni. It struck him upon the head and made an end of him.

So, even at the finish, the boaster made good his boast—no man would ever kill Kalae-puni!

Four Magic Arrows

PIKOI WAS THE SON his father Alala of Kauai had waited
for. Waited many long years while daughter after daughter was
born, until he had six. Then came the seventh child—Pikoi, son
of Alala.

When Pikoi was old enough to decide, he knew what he
wished to be—a bowman, expert with bow and arrow. His father
had scant patience with the idea. The bow was used for little but
rat-shooting, and that was a sport for royalty only. What future
could his son have as a bowman?

But his eldest sister, Beauty of Manoa, having special powers
from the gods, understood his choice. Before she sailed away to
marry Chief Pawaa of Oahu, she gave Pikoi a kapa-wrapped bundle, and in it, four magic arrows.

"Use these arrows well, Pikoi, and one day you will win your
father's approval." She smiled and left.

Years passed, and when Alala felt a longing to see his eldest daughter again, Pikoi was overjoyed to be invited to go with him. He was eager to see again this sister who understood him so well, eager to visit another island.

Tucking his kapa bundle in the laden canoe, Pikoi set out with Alala across the long salt sea to Oahu. They sailed with the wind, paddled without it, and at night slept with a stone anchor to keep them from drifting.

All went well until the last day. Pikoi, paddling in the forward position, heard a cry from his father. Turning, he saw a monster squid slithering over the rear of the canoe, its tentacles reaching for his father.

Pikoi flung open his kapa bundle and drew out an arrow. Fitting it to his bow he took careful aim and let it fly, straight into the ugly body of the monster squid.

His father declared:

"This is Pikoi, son of Alala!
Pikoi, champion bowman of Kauai!
Pikoi of the monster-slaying arrow!"

Pikoi, warmed by his father's first words of praise, picked up his paddle again. They reached the shores of Oahu and made their way to the home of Chief Pawaa and his wife, Beauty of Manoa.

Chief Pawaa looked on smiling at the joyful reunion of father and daughter, brother and sister.

"How is the young bowman?" Pikoi's sister asked.

"Watch," said Pikoi. He sent an arrow straight and true into the bole of a distant palm tree.

"You use your arrows well indeed," said his sister.

"Ae, he does," said his father. "But for Pikoi, I might not be here today." He told them of the monster squid.

Chief Pawaa glanced at his wife and said thoughtfully, "King

Kakuhi-hewa's royal rat-shooting is in progress. I think Pikoi should attend."

Soon Pikoi was on his way with father and brother-in-law. As they neared the field he heard enthusiastic shouts. "Maikai! Hana hou, Mainele! Good! Do it again, Mainele!"

Pikoi saw the bowman Mainele, tall and muscular, step back proudly. He heard the king, laughing, say to his wife, "Well, my Queen, your bowman has lost you the Valley of Manoa. Too bad, but no one can stand against my bowman, Mainele."

Chief Pawaa spoke respectfully. "May I offer the Queen the services of my young brother-in-law Pikoi, just come from Kauai?"

The king nodded, jovially. The queen looked pleased. Mainele scowled. "This stripling?" he scoffed. "I do not compete with children!"

"Do you fear my youth, Mainele?" Pikoi asked. He turned. "May I shoot for you, O Queen?"

"Can you win back the Valley of Manoa?"

"I can," said Pikoi.

"My Coconut Grove of Kailua against the Valley of Manoa," said the queen. "Pikoi to be my bowman."

"Agreed," said the king.

Scowling still, Mainele faced Pikoi. The king announced conditions of the competition. "Each bowman will shoot where his opponent directs. The first to catch fourteen rats will be declared winner. Son of the soil to shoot first."

Mainele took his place, fitted an arrow to his bow, and waited sullenly for Pikoi's direction.

"There. Beside the kamani tree," said Pikoi. "A swarm of rats."

Mainele shot. A cheer went up. The king's servant, retrieving the arrow, held it aloft with three rats dangling from its shaft.

"Only three?" said Pikoi. "I expected ten."

"I'll give you ten!" Mainele cried. Angrily he let fly another arrow. When the servant held it up, it held the ten rats Mainele had promised.

The crowd roared. "See that! Thirteen rats in two shots!" "Mainele needs but one more to win!"

The queen sent an anxious glance at Pikoi. He nodded reassuringly.

Mainele spoke scornfully. "Can you find me one more rat? Or have I shot them all?"

"One hides in the weed patch," Pikoi answered. "Let us see you shoot him through the whiskers."

"I am a champion rat shooter!" Mainele cried. "I have shot rats in the foreleg and in the hind leg. I have shot them through the ear and through the eye. But no one has ever shot a rat through the whiskers!"

"Then watch," said Pikoi. He selected one of his three arrows, took aim, and let fly.

There came a frantic squeaking from the weed patch. The queen's servant, retrieving Pikoi's arrow, held it high for all to see. Impaled upon its shaft were fourteen rats, the last one shot through the whiskers.

The king turned to Pawaa. "This young brother-in-law of yours has cost me the Valley of Manoa but I am happy to know we have such a champion bowman on our island."

The queen thanked Pikoi warmly. Many strangers congratulated him on his marksmanship. But Pikoi felt Mainele's burning eyes follow him as he left the field.

Now that Pikoi had seen Oahu, he longed to see another island. One day, walking along the beach with his brother-in-law after target practice, he saw two canoes approaching. One carried the proud red sail of a high chief, and had many paddlers. The other had a small sail of matting and but a single paddler.

"Let us go to the landing place," Pikoi said eagerly. He and Pawaa watched the canoes come ashore. A runner stepped from the large canoe.

"Can you direct me to the king's residence?" he asked.

Pawaa went off to show the runner the way. Pikoi went down to talk with the lone paddler from the second canoe. His name was Waiakea, he learned. The canoes were from the island of Hawaii, whose High Chief Keawe-nui, in need of an expert bow-man, had sent for Mainele.

Pikoi's eyes gleamed. A chance to visit another island! When Mainele returned with the runner and Pawaa, Pikoi ran to him.

"Mainele, will you take me with you? Perhaps I can help."

Mainele answered scornfully, "The high chief has sent for me! I need no help from you!" He took his place in the large canoe, its sail was hoisted, and it moved swiftly off.

Pikoi, disappointed, watched it go.

Waiakea spoke up. "I could use a paddler. But I must leave at once."

Pikoi glanced at Pawaa, who nodded.

"You have your paddler!" Pikoi said. Storing his bow and arrows in the canoe, he helped push off. A cheerful wave to Pawaa and he was on his way.

Pikoi helped Waiakea raise the small sail. They skimmed through the water with the wind, paddled when it died, straining to put distance behind them; the long miles between Oahu and Molokai, the weary miles between Molokai and Maui, and the gruelling miles between Maui and Hawaii.

They talked little until, nearing their destination, they slowed their pace. "This Mainele is an expert bowman," Waiakea observed.

"He is."

"Have you ever shot against him?"

"I have, and won," said Pikoi.

Waiakea looked startled. "The high chief has heard of Mainele. How is it he has not heard of you?"

"My home is on far Kauai," Pikoi answered. "My father and I came only recently to Oahu for a visit."

Waiakea considered this, then spoke. "When we reach Hilo, stay with me. I will take you up to the forest for the bird-shooting. Then, who knows?"

"My thanks," said Pikoi, and paddled with renewed energy.

They reached Hilo at last. Mainele was there ahead of them but the bird-shooting party would not leave for the forest until morning.

Waiakea took Pikoi home with him, pointing out a fine beach where he might swim before their evening meal.

Eagerly Pikoi plunged in, floating with closed eyes, letting the cool salt water draw the weariness from his aching muscles.

There came a warning cry. A figure on a surf board swept past him and a huge wave boiled over him. He came up sputtering and saw a graceful young girl ride in to shore, turn her board about, and come paddling out to meet him.

"Are you hurt?" she asked.

Pikoi shook his head ruefully. "Only my pride."

The girl smiled—and Pikoi, who had given no thought to maidens, found himself captivated by this one. They swam and surfed together. She asked about his journey and he told her of his trip from Oahu, his visit from Kauai. But when they parted he knew nothing about her but her name—Hokulani.

Next morning, Pikoi and Waiakea joined the crowd following

the royal party to the forest. Pikoi's thoughts turned to Hokulani. He decided to seek her out after the shooting match and learn if she was promised. It was time to think of taking a wife, and Hokulani was the one he wanted.

He followed Waiakea in silence. Higher and higher they climbed until they entered a great koa forest.

Pikoi looked in awe at the canoe trees, their trunks straight and tall, their wood strong and flawless, their crescent leaves rustling in the mountain breeze.

The party came to a clearing where several trees lay felled, and halted. The high chief's kahuna studied the growing trees, chose a towering one, and began his ritual chant.

A derisive call broke the solemn stillness. Glancing up, Pikoi saw two elepaio birds high in the branches begin pecking at the wood.

The kahuna broke off his chant and a groan went up from the crowd. "Just as before!" someone muttered. "Each time, the kahuna chooses a perfect tree. Each time, the birds mark it as flawed."

Pikoi knew that building a canoe was a sacred undertaking, that the kahuna must choose a tree without blemish. If an elepaio bird, which fed on small insects and caterpillars, pecked at the tree, it was unfit for canoe-making.

Pikoi was puzzled. He turned to the man standing near him. "Why this concern? The elepaio birds are doing only what is expected of them."

The man shook his head. "There is something strange about these two birds. They have rejected every tree chosen in the past month, even those which later proved to be flawless. The high chief feels these are kupua birds sent by an enemy to keep him from building more canoes."

Pikoi nodded. Such a thing could be. Kupua were known to

take many different forms. If these were kupua birds, Mainele's arrows would be powerless against them. And what of his own?

Mainele was drawing his bow now, leaning far back and trying to take aim against the dazzling sun. He shot. The shot went wild. The birds squawked, circled, and settled back.

Mainele tried again. His arrow traveled only half the distance to the birds. Their mocking cry sounded again.

Another arrow. Another failure. This time, the birds remained brazenly on their branch. High chief, kahuna, and bowman consulted. Men were sent running to cut saplings and erect a tower beside the tree.

When finished, the tower stood half as high as the great koa and had a platform at its top.

Mainele, bow and arrows slung over his shoulder, slowly climbed to the platform. Leaning back, he took careful aim. Before he could loose his arrow the birds flew to a higher branch, almost out of sight. Mainele's bowstring twanged, the arrow flew high into the air, then fell harmlessly to the ground. Another groan went up from the watchers. Keawe-nui motioned and Mainele sullenly climbed down.

"Now is your chance," Waiakea whispered to Pikoi. "I will speak for you." He went forward and whispered to an attendant, who whispered to another, until the message reached Keawe-nui. There was a stranger here, a bowman who wished to try his luck with the birds.

"Who is this bowman?" Keawe-nui demanded.

Pikoi stepped forward. Keawe-nui eyed him sceptically. The kahuna stared forbiddingly. Mainele, recognizing him, glared.

The high chief spoke. "Every bowman on this island has tried to shoot these wretched birds. Who are you to think you can succeed where they have failed?"

Pikoi made answer:

"I am Pikoi, son of Alala;
Pikoi, champion bowman of Kauai.
Pikoi of the magic arrows:
The monster-slaying arrow,
The rat-slaying arrow,
The bird-slaying arrow,
And the secret arrow."

Keawe-nui shrugged. "You will have need of magic arrows for these birds. Try. Use the tower, if you wish."

Pikoi shook his head. "I need but a large calabash of water."

Keawe-nui frowned but ordered a servant to bring a large calabash and fill it from the royal water gourd.

Pikoi opened his kapa bundle, carefully selected one of the two remaining arrows. Bow in hand, he approached the calabash. Silence spread over the watchers; an unfriendly silence, a cold cynical silence.

The birds still perched in the topmost branches. The sun still blazed overhead. But Pikoi was not bothered by either, for he was not staring up at the birds. He was watching their reflection in the still clear water in the calabash. Slowly he fitted his arrow in place, said a silent prayer to his god, then aiming overhead but keeping his eyes fixed on the birds in his water mirror, he released his arrow.

Swiftly it sped through the air. Swiftly it flew to the treetop. Swiftly it found its target. The two kupua birds fell dead at Keawe-nui's feet.

A great shout went up. Keawe-nui beamed. The kahuna lost his forbidding look. Cold unfriendly eyes grew warm. Only Mainele's scowl remained unchanged.

"Excellent shooting, my young friend," said the high chief. "Let us return to Hilo for a feast to celebrate this happy occasion. There you will receive the prize promised to the winner."

The royal party started down the trail. "What is this prize?" Pikoi asked Waiakea.

"I have not heard," Waiakea answered. "I will ask."

Pikoi walked slowly, lost in happy daydreams. He had visited the island of Hawaii, outshot its best bowmen, met the charming Hokulani, and now was to receive the high chief's gift. What would it be? A canoe? Land? Position? No matter. Whatever it was, he would have something to offer Hokulani.

Waiakea came hurrying back. "Congratulations, my friend! The prize is the high chief's daughter in marriage!"

Pikoi stood stunned. A royal wife! Just as he had found Hokulani! He made the trip down in silence.

The feast was one to remember. Fat pigs, steaming from the imu. Tender white fish, broiled in ki leaves. Tasty young opihi, gathered from the rocks. Yams, coconuts, bananas. But the fine rich food seemed tasteless to Pikoi. His eyes strayed to the women's eating house in the distance. Was Hokulani inside?

The feast ended. High chief and crowd moved to the long house, where dancers and musicians waited, where the women were allowed to join them.

Pikoi searched the crowd for Hokulani, started toward her, then stopped. What could he say? "I hoped to marry you but I have won the high chief's daughter instead"? Slowly he followed Waiakea inside.

Keawe-nui beckoned Pikoi to a place beside him. "A dance to honor our young bowman, Pikoi of Kauai!" he announced.

Four young men leaped to their feet. To the beating of the coconut drum, the slapping of the gourd, they performed a dance that told of kupua birds and a magic arrow. The crowd applauded.

"And now The Chiefess Hula, performed by my daughter," said Keawe-nui.

Pikoi looked up, caught another glimpse of Hokulani, then lost her in the crowd. A maiden had taken her place before the musicians and begun her dance. Pikoi glanced impatiently at her and saw her mischievous smile. Hokulani and the high chief's daughter were one! Pikoi breathed a quiet prayer of thankfulness to his god. To think that Mainele might have won her instead!

Pikoi returned to Oahu with his lovely young bride Hokulani. There was great rejoicing among his kinsmen. But not among the followers of Mainele. Many of them had wagered heavily on Mainele's success with Keawe-nui's birds; wagered and lost. They watched Pikoi resentfully and plotted revenge, waiting only for the right moment. Soon it came.

King Kakuhi-hewa and his queen warmly welcomed Pikoi and his bride, for Pikoi had brought honor to the island by his outstanding archery. They invited the young couple to go surfing with the royal party—an honor, but a dangerous one. Stern kapu governed any activity in which king and queen took part. No one went into the surf before them; no one rode the same wave as they. These were but two of the many forbidden things. Pikoi knew these restrictions, had learned them in childhood, and Hokulani, daughter of a high chief, knew them also.

After a time of surfing, the king and queen came out of the water to rest, giving permission for the others to continue.

For Pikoi and Hokulani there were no others; no royal party, no commoners, just the two of them and the sea. Again and again they paddled out, rode skillfully in.

Later, as they sat their boards beyond the surf, resting, a youth called Apiki swam out. "Pikoi," he called. "A message from the queen. She will catch the first wave. You are to follow on the second. I will tell you when."

When the queen commanded, you obeyed. Pikoi shrugged, smiled at Hokulani, swung his board into position and waited for Apiki's signal. Far to his right he saw the queen plunge into the water, paddle out with her board and sit, waiting. He saw her choose her wave, rise with it, and start her ride.

"Now!" cried Apiki.

Pikoi caught the rising wave as it swelled beneath him, sprang to his feet, and balanced. Behind him he heard Hokulani cry out. Glancing to his right, he saw with dismay that he was riding the far end of the queen's wave! Apiki had tricked him. Quickly he tried to cut out of the wave and fall back, but it was too strong for him. Swiftly it bore him in toward shore.

There, waiting for his arrival, stood Mainele's followers. As he swept in they cried, "Pikoi has broken the kapu! Death to Pikoi!" They fell upon him, kicking, beating, trying to force his head beneath water.

The king, aroused by the tumult, came striding down the beach. "Hold!" he cried. "What happens here?"

Apiki cried out, "This one has broken the queen's kapu! He has ridden the queen's wave! He should die!"

The king turned coldly to Pikoi. "You know the kapu—and the penalty."

Two figures broke from the crowd—Chief Pawaa and Alala, carrying Pikoi's kapa bundle.

"O King, may I speak?" Chief Pawaa requested.

The king nodded.

"I saw it all," Pawaa said. "Pikoi did indeed break the kapu but he acted innocently. Mainele's followers plotted against him for revenge. Apiki directed him onto the queen's wave deliberately, instead of the following one."

The king turned in wrath upon the plotters. "Is this how we

repay a visitor who brings honor to our island? Is this Oahu's sportsmanship? Death shall be yours! You, Pikoi, shall carry out the sentence."

Pikoi came from the water, took from his father his kapa bundle, and unwrapped his last arrow—the secret arrow.

Fitting it to his bow, he aimed and let it fly. Swift and straight it flew to Apiki, struck him down and flew on, from one plotter to the next. When all the treacherous group lay dead upon the sand, the arrow returned to Pikoi's hand to be replaced in his kapa bundle.

The king and queen left. Pikoi took Hokulani by the hand. It was time to pack their belongings and return to Kauai—Kauai, island of the western sea, home of his childhood, home of his family, future home of his bride. Pikoi's four magic arrows had done their work.

The Great Flood

ONCE IN Land Beneath the Sea, there lived the god of fishing, Ku-ula-of-the-Abundant-Sea and his sister, Sea-Maid-of-the-Corals. They had many brothers but these were seldom at home, preferring to change into paoo fish and go frolicking in far waters.

Theirs was a beautiful world, with undersea caverns of rainbow-hued fish, forests of waving water plants, and gardens of delicate coral. Ku-ula and his sister were happy there until one day Ku-ula, swimming near shore, fell in love with a mortal maiden, Hina-of-the-Seashore.

He tried to forget her but could not, so he determined to win her as his wife, even though it meant giving up some of his godly powers and living on earth as a mortal.

His sister, Sea Maid, was filled with sadness when Ku-ula told her of his plans, and begged him to take her with him.

"Wait here for me," he counseled. "If I find it safe, I will send for you." With that she had to be content.

So Ku-ula took on human form, went ashore, and applied as fisherman to the high chief of the district, Koni-konia. The young chief was very fond of fishing, and Ku-ula who with his godly powers could bring fish swarming at will, soon became the chief's head fisherman and his companion, as well.

Ku-ula learned that Hina-of-the-Seashore was one of two daughters of an attendant of the chief. When he was sure of the chief's approval, he decided to ask permission to court her. Just as he was about to bring up the subject, Ku-ula was interrupted by one of the chief's fishermen.

"A strange happening!" said the fisherman. "Two days past we fished above the coral reef and lost our best fish hooks. The line was cut by a sharp piece of coral, we thought. Yesterday we returned. The same thing happened. This time the lines were cleanly cut. Today, I lost my shining turtle-shell hook. I examined the line carefully. Lo, the hook had been removed, not cut! How could such a thing be?"

Puzzled, the chief looked to Ku-ula for comment and saw a strange look on his face. "We will talk more of this later," he told the fisherman and sent him off. Then he turned to Ku-ula. "You know something of this. Tell me."

Ku-ula nodded. "Your fishermen have been casting their lines into Land Beneath the Sea. Until I came here, that was my home."

"What brought you here?"

"Love for one of your people, the maiden Hina-of-the-Seashore," Ku-ula answered. "I hope to win her as my wife."

The young chief nodded. "Tell me more of this Land Beneath the Sea. Who else lives there?"

"My brothers and my sister, Sea-Maid-of-the-Corals," said Ku-ula. "I fear it is she who took your hooks. I promised to send for her. Now she grows impatient."

"I would know more of this maiden," the chief said eagerly. "Is she promised?"

Ku-ula shook his head. "No. She has seen no man but her brothers. She is gentle and soft-spoken, fond of bright things— like your gleaming fish hooks."

"Could she live on land?"

"She could, if she were happy here," Ku-ula replied. "Shall I go and fetch her?"

"No, wait," said Koni-konia. "I would woo her myself. I have a plan. In a few days we shall talk of it."

For the next few days Ku-ula saw little of the chief but sounds of great activity came from the royal enclosure. Then Koni-konia sent for him.

"What do you think of them?" the chief asked. He pointed to a procession of carved wooden images, each with gleaming pearl shell eyes. They ranged in size from one to one small enough to hold in the hand, to one man-size, and each bore a noticeable re-semblance to the young chief himself.

Koni-konia told Ku-ula of his plan and the two set out in the royal canoe. When they reached the coral reef, the chief ordered the canoe to a halt. Then, fastening the smallest image to his line, he lowered it carefully over the side.

Minutes passed. On shore, waves crashed with a hollow boom-ing sound. In the distance a seabird cried.

Then, a sharp tug, and the chief, smiling, drew up an empty line. "Turn about and paddle four canoe-lengths toward shore," he directed his paddlers. They complied.

Koni-konia lowered another image, this one a little larger than the first. Another wait. Another tug. Another smile.

The chief repeated the process again . . . and again . . . and again . . . until the canoe reached the landing place. Then, order-

ing the larger images carried ashore, he placed them at intervals across the sandy beach leading to the royal enclosure. When the last image was set up, the chief took his place a few feet beyond. The paddlers he dismissed. Ku-ula he asked to hide.

The sun shone down on the sandy beach. Small wavelets gently lapped the shore. The chief stood motionless, eyes fixed on the sea.

Then, a faint splash. Something stirred in the water beyond the quiet bay. Stirred again, a few yards nearer. . . and again, nearer still.

The chief gave a small cry of delight as a slim form broke from the water in a spray of sparkling droplets. Sea-Maid-of-the-Corals ran up the beach to the first carved figure planted in the sand and touched the wooden arms with gentle hands. Then, with a joyful laugh, she ran on to the next . . . to the next.

Koni-konia held his breath. Sea Maid was just a few feet away. Smiling, she came toward him, touched his arm, then drew back with a startled cry. She turned to flee and Koni-konia called to Ku-ula for help.

"My sister, wait!" Ku-ula cried. Leaving his hiding place, he started toward her. Reassured, she turned back and ran to meet him.

Briefly Ku-ula explained, presented Sea Maid to the chief, who invited her to stay and visit with her brother.

It was a happy time for Sea Maid. As the days passed she explored this new land with growing wonder. When, in time, Koni-konia asked her to become his wife, she accepted.

The young chief, eager to share his new-found happiness, paved the way for Ku-ula with the parents of Hina-of-the-Seashore, and soon Ku-ula had the young wife he had admired from afar.

The days passed quickly. Then one morning a fisherman came

running to report a very high tide and school of paoo fish leaping from the water.

Hastily Ku-ula cancelled the day's fishing, sent word to Sea Maid, and ran to rescue Hina. "Run to high ground!" he urged everyone he passed on the way. Soon he saw the chief and Sea Maid hurry with their attendants for the hills. The villagers followed. With his wife, Ku-ula joined them.

From the hilltop, they watched the waters rising. "We must climb the mountain!" Sea Maid cried. "My brothers are trying to carry me back to Land Beneath the Sea!"

Everyone climbed higher. Far up the mountainside, as they stopped to rest, they saw muddy waters wash away their canoes, their farms, their trees, their homes. Still the waters continued to rise.

"Climb trees!" Ku-ula ordered. Everyone found a safe place high in the branches but still the waters continued to rise. Ku-ula left his wife and went to the very edge of the rising water.

"Listen my brothers!" he called. "Our sister has found a good husband, and I a good wife. We are happy here in Land Above the Sea. Leave us in peace."

As all watched fearfully, the waters grew calm. Slowly they began to recede. Koni-konia and his people were left staring at their ruined village. Sea Maid wept bitterly.

Ku-ula returned. "Dry your tears, my sister," he said. "What the people of the sea have destroyed, the people of the land will rebuild." With Hina at his side, he led the way down the mountainside into the ruined village and set to work.

Not a dwelling, not a tree was left standing, but not a life was lost. Ku-ula's neighbors, grateful for their deliverance, set to work with a will. Soon new grass houses appeared, new gardens sprouted, new trees sprang up.

Before long all traces of the great flood were lost in the new growth, but the memory did not fade. Events were dated from the time of the Great Flood, and the story was told to each new child as he came of age.

The Empty Sea

AFTER THE GREAT FLOOD, Ku-ula-of-the-Abundant-Sea and his wife Hina-of-the-Seashore decided it was time to move on. They set out for the district of Hana, on the island of Maui, where Ku-ula found employment as fisherman to Shark Chief.

Ku-ula's special powers with fish soon brought his promotion to head fisherman. He built a great fishpond for Shark Chief and fish swarmed into it, bringing fame to the chief throughout the island. Ku-ula soon won a place of respect in his new home. There, in a section of Hana known as Alea-wai, his son Aiai was born and grew up happily, playing with a neighbor's boy named Pili.

As Aiai grew, Ku-ula taught him more and more of his own special fishing lore. One day as they were preparing their fishing lines, Ku-ula said, "Today is an important occasion. We are going out to deep water to fish for aku with the Fish-hook-come-from-heaven." He showed Aiai a hook made from gleaming pearl shell. As it flashed in the sunlight, a sleek white bird flew in from the sea and lighted on Ku-ula's shoulder. Aiai stared in amazement.

His father spoke fondly to the bird. "This is Seabird," he explained. "He is special guardian of this fish-hook. The head of the first fish we catch is for him."

When they had pushed their canoe into the water and hoisted its matting sail, Seabird flew to the prow and settled there. When they reached the aku fishing ground, he took flight and circled close to the water with strange excited cries.

"He has sighted fish," Ku-ula said. "Cast your line."

Aiai cast, and almost as soon as his hook touched water he felt a great tug, and pulled in a fine aku. Cutting off its head, he placed it on the prow for Seabird, who returned and perched there as he ate. Aku came leaping into the canoe and in a very short time, Ku-ula and Aiai had all the fish needed for the chief's household and their own, and so they returned to shore.

They had just beached their canoe when a messenger came running with a report that fish were disappearing from the chief's royal fishpond. Ku-ula sent Aiai home with the family share of fish and went to look into the matter.

He learned that the pond-keeper had seen a monstrous eel with fierce teeth slip in through the sea gate of the royal fishpond and make a meal of the chief's fish. The keeper, trying to catch him with a baited line, had been pulled into the pond where he lost a foot to the vicious intruder.

This was no ordinary eel. Ku-ula, with his special powers, recognized Great Eel, a kupua chief from the island of Molokai.

Summoning the people of Alea-wai and the people of Hane-o-o, he fastened his special bait stick to his line and attached his Fish-hook-come-from-heaven. He tied his line to the middle of a long stout rope and gave an end to each group with orders to pull when he gave the signal. Then he dropped his line into the fishpond and waited.

Soon there came a powerful tug. Great Eel had swallowed hook and line and dived deep, bracing himself between two strong rocks of the sea gate.

Ku-ula gave the signal. On opposite sides of the fishpond, the people of Alea-wai and the people of Hane-o-o pulled in a furious tug-of-war. The rope strained to one side, then to the other, but Great Eel gave not an inch. On and on went the struggle, until Great Eel was torn in two and Ku-ula retrieved his Fish-hook come-from-heaven.

After that, no more fish disappeared from the chief's fishpond. But back on Molokai, news of Great Eel's death reached his vengeful follower Panai, who came secretly to Hana and found employment under Shark Chief, as messenger.

The weeks went by and Panai served quietly. Then he came one day to the fishpond where Ku-ula was working, with word that Shark Chief wished an ulua fish for his household. It was a time of great scarcity of ulua in that area, and Ku-ula had but a single one in the royal fishpond. He took it out and gave it to Panai with careful instructions for its preparation.

"Tell the chief the head should be cut off and dried in the sun, the body baked in the imu, for it will be many days before the people of Hana see another such fish."

This was Panai's opportunity. He carried the fish to Shark Chief and said, "Your head fisherman, Ku-ula, gave me a strange message for you. He said that your head should be cut off and dried in the sun, your body baked in the imu, for it will be many days before the people of Hana see another such chief."

Shark Chief, in great wrath and without inquiring into the matter, ordered all his people to gather firewood and place it around the home of Ku-ula, for he and his wife and son were to be burned to death.

The people of Alea-wai, Ku-ula's neighbors, were horrified at the cruel order and took no part in carrying it out. They went secretly to a distant fishing place and pretended not to have heard Shark Chief's order.

But the rest of the people obeyed, piling wood high about the house of the head fisherman. Ku-ula was bound to the end post of his house, Hina-of-the-Seashore to the middle post, and Aiai to the corner post.

Soon the crackling of flames could be heard outside. Then Ku-ula gave directions to his son. "When the smoke rises, your mother and I will return to the sea. I leave you my fishing calabash and in it my four magic talismans: my bait stick, my cowrie shell, my water-washed pebbles, my stone image. You know how to use them. When the smoke blows toward the mountain your ropes will drop off. Slip out through the curtain of smoke and make your way up the mountainside. Find a cave and hide until it is safe to be seen again."

Soon the smoke began to rise and Aiai saw his father and mother drift through the doorway and disappear. He watched until the smoke blew toward the mountain and felt the ropes drop from his arms and legs. Then with his father's fishing calabash in his arms, Aiai slipped out through the curtain of smoke, made his way up the mountainside, and hid himself in a cave.

The people of Alea-wai, returning from their fishing trip, saw the smouldering ruins of Ku-ula's house, and wept.

As they stood weeping, they saw a rippling of the wind on the sea, saw a misty rain sweep inland and, strangely, fan the dying sparks into leaping flames that reached out into the crowd and consumed all who had obeyed Shark Chief's orders.

When the rain had ended and the fire had died, none remained but Shark Chief and the people of Alea-wai, who wondered bit-

terly why such a cruel chief should live while all who had followed his orders had died.

Aiai remained hidden in his mountain cave for several days
then, before daybreak, made his way to the home of his friend
Pili. Pili rejoiced to see him, having thought him dead, but when
Aiai asked for food, he shook his head sadly.

"Aiai, my people are starving," he answered. "The sea is empty
of fish, the rocks bare of crab, the streams drained of shrimp. It is
as though your father took them all with him when he died. Shark
Chief demands hinalea and threatens death if we do not provide
them. Tell me, how are we to catch fish from an empty sea?"

"I will help you, Pili," said Aiai. "Take my special bait stick
and fasten it to your basket. When you lower it to the sea bottom,
hinalea will return. Leave two of your catch at the fishing shrine
and take the remainder to Shark Chief."

With Aiai's help, Pili caught the hinalea needed to save his
people. He left two at the fishing shrine and delivered the remainder to Shark Chief who, too greedy to wait for them to be
skinned or cooked, wolfed the first one down raw. Its scales caught
in his throat and strangled him—a fitting end, thought Pili.

With Shark Chief gone and hinalea returned, life was peace-
ful again in Alea-wai. One day as Aiai and Pili pounded bait for
their fish traps, Pili spoke wistfully. "Hinalea have returned to
our waters and we are indeed fortunate. Yet there are times when
I yearn for the taste of squid."

Aiai said, "Pili, this is what you must do. Take this special
cowrie-shell lure. Fasten it to your line and move it along the sea
bottom. Teach your fishermen to do the same. Soon you will have
your squid. But pay heed! Do not leave the cowrie in the sea too
long or the salt water will dull its gleam and it will attract squid
no longer."

Pili did as Aiai directed and all went well. Each fisherman made his own squid lure and no man fished too long or took too many.

Now the waters swarmed with squid and the people of Alea-wai were content. But not for long. Soon they wished for something more, and sent Pili to speak for them.

"Aiai, my friend," said Pili, "my people now have squid in plenty, and they thank you, but. . . ."

"Yes?"

"They long for the taste of the big-eyed red fish, aweoweo."

Aiai said, "Pili, this is what you must do. Take these four water-washed pebbles. Drop them from your canoe just beyond the breakers. Teach your fishermen to do the same. Soon the fish will have a resting place and when you cast your line you will catch aweoweo. But pay heed! Set aside a kapu period when no fish may be taken, so the waters will not be fished out."

Pili did as Aiai directed and all went well. Each time a fisherman took his canoe out, he dropped four water-washed pebbles at the spot beyond the breakers and soon the big-eyed red fish crowded to the spot, and when the kapu flag flew he took no fish at all.

Now the waters swarmed with aweoweo and the people of Alea-wai were content. But not for long. Soon they wished for something more and sent Pili to speak for them.

"Aiai, my friend," said Pili, "my people now have aweoweo in plenty, and they thank you, but. . . ."

"Yes?"

"They miss the scampering rock crab."

Aiai said, "Pili, this is what you must do. Take this stone image, set it on the rocks, and pray to the god of fishing. Teach your fishermen to do the same. Soon you will have your rock crab. But pay heed! Do not take all you can find. Leave some to grow and multiply."

Pili did as Aiai directed and all went well. Each fisherman set up his own stone image and prayed to the god of fishing for rock crab, and each time he gathered, he left some to grow and multiply.

Now with the waters swarming with squid, aweoweo, and rock crab, the people of Alea-wai should have been content. But who was ever content for long? Soon they wished for something more and sent Pili to speak for them.

But this time, Pili found it difficult, and stood before Aiai, tongue-tied.

So Aiai spoke. "Pili, my friend," he said, "Your people now have rock crab in plenty, and they thank me, but . . . there is one thing more. True?"

"True," Pili answered, shame-faced.

"And that?"

"They crave the little freshwater shrimp they once gathered from the mountain stream."

Aiai nodded. "Pili, tell your people that when the next rain falls the shrimp will return to the mountain stream. Then each family may gather them again, but only a single calabash to a family!"

Pili did as Aiai directed. But when the next rain fell and he went to the mountain stream, he saw with dismay men, women, and children rushing about, filling calabashes, setting them on the bank, then plunging in to fill more. Pili felt shame at their greed and called out to remind them of Aiai's warning, but they paid no heed.

Then, all at once, the shrimp disappeared from the stream. But the people laughed. Had they not all those full calabashes on the bank? Each man, woman, and child gathered up his own catch to carry home. Each found his calabash filled, not with shrimp but with wriggling lizards. Screaming, they threw them away, and ran.

Aiai, hearing what had happened, bid Pili summon the people to the long house. There he appeared and spoke.

"People of Alea-wai, you knew my father as neighbor and head fisherman to Shark Chief. You did not know him in his true form, Ku-ula-of-the-Abundant-Sea, god of fishing."

A fearful moan went up from the people.

Aiai explained. "When Shark Chief ordered us burned to death, we did not die. My father and mother walked out upon the smoke and returned to the sea, taking with them all fish and seafood. You were saved because you took no part in Shark Chief's act, and my father left me his magic talismans to restore the fish and seafood if you proved worthy."

"Auwe!" cried the people, filled with guilt.

Aiai went on. "You asked for squid and squid returned. You asked for aweoweo and aweoweo returned. You asked for rock crab and rock crab returned. These you used wisely and all went well. Then you asked for shrimp and shrimp returned. But these you did not use wisely. You became greedy and took all you could catch, and so my father Ku-ula turned your shrimp into lizards."

"Auwe!" mourned the people, overcome by shame.

Aiai concluded. "The time has come for me to travel about the islands, doing the work Ku-ula left for me to do. I appoint Pili as your head fisherman. He knows what should be done to conserve the fishing grounds. Do as he says and all will be well. Disregard him and the fish will disappear again, and this time Ku-ula will not return them."

So Aiai took his leave. Pili served faithfully as head fisherman, and the people followed his teachings.

When they fished for squid, they caught only a reasonable

number, then drew up their cowrie-shell lures. When they fished for aweoweo, they added pebbles to the fishes' resting place and when the kapu flag flew they took no fish at all. When they gathered rock crab, they left some to grow and multiply. When they gathered shrimp, each family filled but a single calabash and left the rest to replenish the stream.

Soon the fishing grounds of Alea-wai became known as the finest in the islands. Whenever a stranger asked one of their fishermen his secret, he smiled and answered, "Ku-ula, god of fishing, has been good to us. He taught us how to bring back an abundant sea from what was once for us an empty sea."

The Pearl Fish-hook

YOUNG AIAI, son of the god of fishing, was married to Ka-ua, daughter of the Chief of Honolulu, and lived on the island of Oahu. As the years passed, Aiai longed to see again his father Ku-ula.

Whenever Aiai met a stranger he asked the same question. "In your travels have you met a fisherman named Ku-ula?" and the answer was always the same. "I have not."

Then came a day when the answer was different. A traveler returning from Maui reported having seen a lonely old man called Ku-ula in a small fishing village. Day after day he sat by the sea with an ailing seabird for companion.

Aiai turned the matter over and over in his mind. A lonely old man sitting by the sea? That surely did not sound like his father Ku-ula, god of fishing. But the seabird companion? That did.

Aiai decided he must see for himself. He bade farewell to his wife, Ka-ua, and set out for the island of Maui. As he traveled, his thoughts turned back to the early days of fishing with his father and Seabird; to the day when he had first seen the gleaming Fish-hook-come-from-heaven, that brought aku leaping into their canoe.

Aiai found the village described by the traveler, and made inquiries. Yes, there was the man Ku-ula, sitting on the sea wall.

Aiai saw a man staring out to sea, his hand gently stroking the feathers of a scrawny bird nestled beside him. He hurried down.

"Ku-ula?" he called softly.

The man looked up, empty-eyed, then turned back to the sea.

"Ku-ula, my father?" said Aiai.

The man raised his eyes and looked—really looked. "Aiai? My son!" he cried.

"My father, how can this be?" Aiai protested. "You, god of fishing, living in a fishing village and ignored?"

Ku-ula shook his head sadly. "Who believes in a fishing god unable to catch fish?"

"But when I fished with you, the aku leaped into your canoe!" Aiai said.

Ku-ula nodded. "Ae, they did. In those days both Seabird and I were strong and respected. But that was before I lost the Fish-hook-come-from-heaven."

"How could you lose your magic fish-hook, my father? Seabird always took such good care of it!"

"Ae, he did. But it was stolen from its hiding place in the rafters one night as Seabird and I both slept."

"And you have no knowledge of the thief?"

"None," said Ku-ula. "But this I know. No one on this island has it, for there has been no good catch of aku here for many years."

"Would Seabird recognize the hook if he saw it again?"

Ku-ula shrugged. "Ae, if he were well and strong. But look at

him! I can scarcely remember when he had his last taste of aku."

Aiai shook his head in dismay. It was hard to recognize sleek, lusty Seabird in this scrawny, shivering bird with dull feathers and half-closed eyes.

Then Aiai felt a growing excitement within him. "Let me borrow Seabird, my father! I will get aku for him and when he is well again we will search for your pearl fish-hook until we find it!"

Ku-ula's eyes lost their faraway look, and when he bade his son goodbye, he stood tall and walked with his old confidence.

So it was that Aiai returned home bearing an ailing seabird wrapped in a piece of soft kapa cloth. His wife Ka-ua took the bird gently and made a resting place for it. Each day Aiai fed it bits of aku.

Days slipped by and Aiai noticed two happy things: Seabird was growing sleek and strong again, and Ka-ua was expecting a child. As often happens at such times, she developed a strong craving. It was for one thing only—aku. There was nothing Aiai could do about this, for this fish was forbidden to women during pregnancy. Aiai joked about his two seabirds with hungry appetites for aku; joked until he saw Ka-ua hungrily eyeing Seabird's portion. Then he grew fearful, knowing that for any pregnant woman found eating aku, the penalty was death. He substituted other fish. Since Seabird had regained his strength, the change of diet did not bother him, but Ka-ua grew sad and pale, and Aiai feared for her health and the child's.

It seemed as though her time would never come. Finally, in the month of Kaelo, a son was born. Smiling in their relief, they named him Punia-ka-ia, Craving-for-Fish.

Ka-ua bloomed again. "Now I can have my aku," she said happily.

But Aiai shook his head. "Not yet, my wife. Have you forgotten? There is a kapu on the taking of aku during the month of Kaelo."

The long month dragged by. The dark night of the dying moon came at last. Aiai, preparing his fishing gear, thought eagerly of the aku he would catch for his wife, the Fish-hook-come-from-heaven he would recover for his father.

To observe the lifting of the kapu, Chief Kipapa-ula himself went out with the fishing fleet. Aiai, knowing that no fisherman might paddle close to the chief's canoe, fished at a safe distance, with Seabird on his prow. He was watching his line when he heard a great shout from the chief's canoe and saw aku leaping from the water to take the chief's hook.

Seabird, with a shrill cry, took off, flew to the chief's canoe and circled there, diving whenever the chief cast his line. Kipapa-ula, annoyed by the bird's actions, soon put away his hook and ordered his paddlers to return to shore. Seabird, with harsh cries, followed the royal canoe for some distance, then returned to Aiai.

Although he had caught nothing, Aiai had to return now, for no one might continue fishing without special permission after the high chief had stopped. He followed at a safe distance behind the chief's canoe, and his eyes were troubled.

It was clear from Seabird's actions that he had found the Fish-hook-come-from-heaven. But Chief Kipapa-ula? High Chief of Honolulu? His own father-in-law? Could this be the thief? Yet it was not unbelievable, for a high chief could do no wrong, and the best of everything was thought to be his. At some time he must have seen Ku-ula fishing with the magic hook, seen the aku leaping into the canoe, and desired that fish-hook above all others. It would have been a small matter to have a man follow Ku-ula home and steal the hook while he slept. Many chiefs had specially trained thieves for just such matters.

But how was Aiai to get it back? An answer came when he saw Ka-ua's disappointed face at his return, empty-handed.

"There is a way I could surely get aku for you," he told her. "Your father has a most unusual pearl fish-hook. Today when he used it, the fish leaped to his line. You are his beloved daughter who has just given him his first grandson. If you ask, perhaps he would let me borrow this fish-hook."

Ka-ua went to her father and he reluctantly loaned the hook, reminding her of the importance of returning it safely to its owner.

Before daybreak, Aiai and Seabird were on their way. This day the chief would not be fishing so there was no kapu for others who wished to fish.

Scarcely had they reached deep water when Seabird gave a joyful cry. Aiai fastened the pearl fish-hook to his line and cast. At once he pulled in a fat aku. Cutting off its head and tail for Seabird, he set aside the fish as an offering at the fishing shrine. Aku began leaping from the water all about him. Aiai caught four, then pulled in his line. There was no need to fish any longer. He had found what he was seeking.

Carefully he loosed the gleaming Fish-hook-come-from-heaven and held it out. Seabird took it gently from his hand, and holding it firmly in his beak, rose with a graceful lift of wings.

Seabird circled once, then flew off in a straight line, and Aiai knew his destination. He knew that soon, on the island of Maui, a lonely old man watching the sea would sight Seabird returning with his treasured Fish-hook-come-from-heaven and would be a lonely old man no longer; would be once again Ku-ula-of-the-Abundant-Sea, god of fishing.

Aiai turned homeward. There was aku at last for his wife Ka-ua, and there was also the matter of telling Chief Kipapa-ula that Aiai had indeed returned the pearl fish-hook safely to its owner.

Great Roving Uhu

PUNIA-KA-IA, meaning Craving-for-Fish, was well named, for he longed to be a recognized fisherman, a lawaia.

Many times Punia had gone out in the fishing canoes, but only as a paddler. Ka! That was nothing! Would he get his chance to-day? But he heard the steersman's command, and saw the canoes of the fishing fleet begin to turn about and head for home. No chance today!

Lost in gloomy thought, Punia failed to hear someone call his name. The call came again.

"Punia!"

Punia turned. The head fisherman was holding out the long-awaited pole and line. He took them with murmured thanks. Stealing a glance at his father Aiai seated in the stern, he received an encouraging nod.

Eagerly Punia drew his gleaming pearl fish-hook from the waist-band of his malo and fastened it on his line. He tried to remember all his father had taught him about aku . . . they swam with the current not against it . . . they lived in deep water but were caught at the surface where they came in pursuit of small silvery fish . . . he must draw his hook through the water so it sparkled like these small fish, tempting the aku to bite.

With a silent prayer to his fishing aumakua, Punia tossed his line into the water. The canoes moved steadily on, but no one else cast a line. This was the ritual. He alone was to have his chance.

Punia saw his hook flash and sparkle as it followed the canoe, but nothing happened. After all this time, was he to have his chance and fail for lack of fish?

There came a sudden splash, a tug. Punia flipped his line and there it lay in the bottom of the canoe—his first recognized catch, a fair-sized aku. Carefully, Punia drew his knife, cut off the tail, and placed the fish on the bow of the canoe—his offering for the shrine of the fishing god.

No word was spoken by the other fishermen but their faces grew a little less grim. A look of comradeship passed between Punia and his father. The paddlers increased their pace, for now a special ceremony lay ahead. In his mind, Punia rehearsed his part.

The canoes reached shore and Punia waited for the head fisherman to leave the canoe, then leaped after him. Carrying his fish carefully, he went directly to the fishing shrine and handed his offering to the kahuna. Solemnly he watched as the priest prayed, then cut the fish in small pieces, wrapped them in ki leaves, and set them to cook. His fish would be ready by the time the canoes were unloaded. Then Punia would have the honor of inviting all the men of the fleet to be his guests.

All worked unloading the catch. Then Punia ceremoniously

extended his invitation. All talking ceased. The men of the fishing fleet washed their hands in sea water and silently followed Punia to the shrine.

There lay Punia's fish, cooked and spread upon fresh green ki leaves. The kahuna began his chant:

"Aumakua of the East,
Aumakua of the North,
Aumakua of the West,
Aumakua of the South,
Aumakua of the Great Sea,
Aumakua of the Small Sea,
Behold Punia-ka-ia, young fisherman.
Send him full waters for his fishing:
Swarms of little snub-nosed fishes,
Schools of leaping aku,
Fighting ahi from the ocean depths.
Make him a responsible fisherman.
This is the ending of our prayer.
It is finished."

Then the priest and each of the fishermen received a piece of Punia's fish and ate it in silence. When all had finished, Punia carefully gathered up the bones, wrapped them in a ki leaf, and with a prayer of thanks to his grandfather aumakua, Ku-ula, cast his packet into the sea.

Returning home after the ceremony, Punia heard a splash from the fishpond he had helped his father build. There, leaping up to greet him, was his pet uhu fish.

Punia smiled, remembering how as a boy, impatient with the long wait before he could become a professional fisherman, he had taken his small bamboo pole and played at fishing with his father. To his delight, he had caught a young uhu with bright green body and blue-ringed eyes. Proudly he had placed it in his father's fishpond. There each day he fed it bits of sea moss and chunks of cooked sweet potato. There his pet fish had grown steadily and had become so tame that he would rise to the surface at the sound of Punia's footsteps, Punia's alone. His parents called it Punia's keiki—Punia's child. Whenever Punia wanted it, he chanted:

> "O my keiki uhu,
> Swim this way,
> Swim this way.
> Come along, come along
> To Punia who calls you."

Then the fish would come to him and nuzzle his hand.

Now, Punia stooped to offer the bit of sea moss he had brought for it. "Ho, my keiki," he said. "Today is the great day! I have passed my test! I am now an accepted lawaia! It is time for you to go roving, and what better day than today to set you free?"

Carefully, Punia slipped the fish into a calabash of water, carried him down to the sea, and turned him loose. As he watched him swim away, Punia wondered if he would ever see his keiki uhu again.

The days dragged by. Punia waited eagerly for a summons to join the fishing fleet. None came. He knew from his father the reason. The fish famine, foreseen by the head fisherman, had come upon them. With the sea drained of fish, the head fisherman had ceased to call his men out.

The famine lengthened. The people of the village began to suffer, for much of their food came from the fishing fleet. Now they had only sweet potato and poi, sea moss and seaweed. On such a diet adults grew listless and children fretful.

Then came the summons Punia had waited for. The fleet would make a trip to deep water in hopes of finding fish.

Solemnly Punia helped his father make preparations. There were the fish-hooks to be checked before sundown, placed in their covered gourd containers, and stored high in the rafters, safe from contamination, for no fish would bite on a tainted hook. That was his father's responsibility. There was the family dog to be tied, the family rooster to be placed in a covered calabash, to keep them quiet, for no sound must offend the god of fishing on this important occasion. That was Punia's responsibility.

He was still hungry when he lay down upon his sleeping kapa. His mouth watered for the taste of aku and he prayed that the next day's trip would be successful.

It seemed that he had barely closed his eyes when he felt his father shaking him. Only a pearly gray light showed through the doorway of the sleeping house. His father, finger to lips, motioned for Punia to wash and get ready.

Soon, with fish-hook and knife tucked into the waistband of his malo, Punia accompanied his father to the fishing shrine, joining the other members of the fishing fleet in a petition to Ku-ula for a good catch. Then silently, the shadowy figures made their way to the canoe launching place.

As the sun broke through the eastern portal of the day, the fishing fleet slipped silently out to sea. The morning breeze filled the crab-claw sail and the canoe skimmed through the water until no sign of land remained but the mountain peak from which the steersman took his bearing.

The head fisherman gave a command. It was time for casting. Punia, the youngest fisherman, waited respectfully until all had cast their lines. But he heard no splash, saw no leaping forms following the gleaming hooks.

His father nodded and Punia fastened his own hook in place and made his cast. Nothing happened. The eerie silence raised prickles on the back of his neck. In the distance he heard a faint splash, then silence again.

Something bumped the side of the canoe. Glancing down he saw the bright green body, the blue-ringed eyes of his keiki uhu —a keiki no longer. Reaching into the bait container, Punia held out a morsel. Gently the uhu nibbled it. Then he swirled about and Punia saw with astonishment, two long lines of fish following behind in perfect formation. On and on they came until the water was dark with them. Leaping, they took the hook until the lawaia were flipping them into the canoes as fast as they could lift their lines.

Soon the canoes lay deep in the water with their catch, and the head fisherman gave the command to halt. Punia saw his pet leap from the water, turn about, and swim back the way he had come. Dutifully following went two files of the fish that remained.

Now the kapu of silence was broken. There was laughter and cheerful talk and shouts of congratulations for Punia and his keiki uhu.

Punia grinned. "Keiki uhu no longer!" he retorted. "My great roving uhu!"

A few weeks later, when fish was needed again, Punia went alone to the beach and called:

"O Great Roving Uhu,
Swim this way,
Swim this way!
Come along, come along
To Punia who calls you.
Bring fish in large numbers:
Enough for our god,
Enough for our chief,
Enough for our people."

Great Roving Uhu answered his call, bringing his orderly files of fish swimming behind him until the waters grew dark with their coming.

From that time on, whenever Punia and his people needed fish, he chanted his call to Great Roving Uhu, and because Punia and the men of his village were honorable fishermen, Great Roving Uhu always answered his call.

Young Punia was a highly respected lawaia in his own village, but as he grew to manhood he longed to see other islands. Was fishing good there? Did fishermen use different methods, different hooks, different bait?

But Punia had no sea-going canoe of his own, and his father's was part of the fishing fleet, so his chance of seeing another island seemed slim indeed.

One day he saw four brothers storing provisions in a large sea-going canoe, and asked their destination.

"Kauai," said the eldest. "We go to make a new home there."

"Come with us!" said the youngest. "We would enjoy your company."

His brothers nodded, so Punia accepted. With nothing but the small gourd containing his fish-hooks and line, he set out with the four brothers for the island of Kauai in the western sea.

It was no easy trip from Oahu to Kauai. When the wind died, only their muscles kept them moving, but Punia paddled eagerly. Muli-loa, the youngest brother, chattered steadily, making the time pass more quickly. Muli-loa-of-the-Wagging-Tongue, his brothers called him.

When the island finally came in sight, Punia thought it even more beautiful than he had dreamed: smooth golden beaches, quiet blue bays, rolling green hills.

The sun was dropping into the sea as they arrived. They found a quiet cove, beached their canoe, and plunged into the water for a swim. All were hungry when they came out. The brothers shared their provisions with Punia, then the five stretched out on the sun-warmed sand, exchanging experiences.

Punia told of his keiki uhu who had become the Great Roving Uhu. Muli-loa stared at him in awe. "You are the Punia who saved your village from starvation!" he exclaimed.

Punia laughed. "How would you know of that? Your home was on the far side of the island."

"What matter?" said the boy. "Everywhere on the island they know of Punia and his Great Roving Uhu! Surely Kauai has no fisherman to match you!"

"Who knows?" Punia answered, smiling.

As darkness fell, the five wrapped themselves in kapa covers and slept upon the sand. Before daylight, Punia woke and saw three local fishermen preparing to set out. Eager to compare fishing notes, he slipped from his covers without waking his companions, and joined the group.

"What do you fish for?" he asked.

One of the men looked up sullenly. "Bonefish."

"And there will be few of those," another added.

"How much longer will this fish famine last?" the third complained, shaking his head.

"It will pass," Punia assured them. "We have suffered such a famine on Oahu also."

Muli-loa had quietly joined the group but did not remain quiet for long. "This is Punia who saved his village from starvation!" he announced eagerly. "When no one else could catch a single fish, he brought fish swarming to his canoe!"

The sullen one confronted Punia. "Let us see you work such a miracle here."

Punia, embarrassed, shook his head. "Muli-loa exaggerates."

The second fisherman joined in. "You would save the people of your own island but not ours, eh?"

"Not so," Punia answered. "At home I had help from my Great Roving Uhu. But here. . . ."

The three exchanged glances and closed in on Punia. The sullen one spoke again. "You will catch such a swarm of fish for us or we will take your canoe."

Punia saw the concern in Muli-loa's face and spoke quickly. "I will try," he said. "No man can do more."

"You will do more," said the sullen one. "You will make such a catch or your bones will bake in the earth oven."

Muli-loa grew pale. "Oh, Punia!" he cried. "What have I done?"

"No matter," said Punia. To the sullen one he said, "If I am to wager my bones, it will be against something of value. What do you offer?"

The sullen one considered. "I have a kalo patch . . ."

"Not enough," replied Punia.

"I have another," said the second.

Punia shook his head. "At least four pieces. One for my back, one for my front, one for each side."

The three conferred. "We will put up four parcels of land," they offered.

"And your canoe," said Punia.

"Too much!" they protested. "Without our canoe how are we to make a living?"

"More easily than I without my bones," Punia retorted. "If you cannot afford to wager, let us hear no more of it."

"Wait!" cried the third. To the others he said, "Such a catch during this famine would bring generous recognition from the high chief. . . ."

His companions nodded. "And we could trade our own shares of the catch for another canoe. . . ." the second added.

"But what if he fails?"

The sullen one smiled, an evil smile. "If he fails, we offer him to the high chief for sacrifice. We cannot lose!"

"Ae," the others agreed. "Make the wager."

The conditions were set and agreed upon. The sullen one added, "That you may not think the people of Kauai unreasonable, we give you fifteen days to work your miracle."

The following morning, Punia and his friends set out in their canoe at daybreak. On reaching deep water, Punia began his chant:

> "O Great Roving Uhu,
> Swim this way, swim this way!
> Come along, come along
> To Punia who needs you!
> Bring fish in large numbers:
> Enough for our god,
> Enough for this chief,
> Enough for these people."

Tying on his favorite hook, he cast his line into the sparkling water. Nothing happened. He tried again. The other four tried. Nothing. Not even a bonefish. After weary hours they turned the canoe shoreward. Even Muli-loa was silent.

"Cheer up, my friends," said Punia. "Fourteen days remain."

But eleven of those days went by and the results were the same —not a fish. Punia considered. It could be that my uhu does not hear me from such a distance, he thought. So when on the twelfth day he saw a canoe leaving for Oahu, he sent a message to his parents: "Try to reach Great Roving Uhu! Send him to Kauai. My life depends upon it!"

Slowly, two more days passed, and each day's catch was like the others—nothing. The Kauai fishermen, growing more and more hungry, grew more and more cruel. They watched each day's departing trip with scorn, met each returning trip with jeers.

"Time to build the fire," said one on the fourteenth day. "Tomorrow we fill the imu."

"Too bad," observed the sullen one. "A full oven and none of the meat fit to eat."

Punia found sleep long in coming that last night. Nearby he could hear Muli-loa tossing and turning too. As soon as dawn lighted the sky, Punia threw off his sleeping kapa and made his way to the water's edge. In silence he prayed to his god, then softly began his chant:

> "O Great Roving Uhu,
> Swim this way, swim this way!
> Come along! Come along!
> To Punia who needs you!"

He stopped suddenly. The water had taken on a remembered dark color. The first wave reached shore, broke upon the sand, and receded; receded, leaving hundreds of fish leaping and flapping on the beach.

"Muli-loa! Wake your brothers!" Punia cried. "Call the Kauai fishermen! Our fish have come!"

Punia waded out into the water. Something nudged his leg. There was his Great Roving Uhu.

"Oh, my keiki!" Punia cried. "Never have I needed you more! But for you, today my bones would bake in the imu."

Swarms of people came running to the beach: the four Kauai fishermen . . . their kinsmen . . . their neighbors . . . their friends . . . the high chief's men. Everyone ran about gathering all the fish he could carry. After weeks of famine, now there was fish for

Punia's god, fish for the chief, fish for the people, fish for the imu and the drying rack. There was even fish for the pigs and the dogs.

The Kauai fishermen showed Punia the land he had won. He gave a parcel to each of his friends.

"You bought this land with your life!" they protested. "How can we accept it?"

Punia laughed. "Of what use would it be to me on Oahu? I came only to see the fishing here. You came to make a new home. You can use the land, I can use the canoe."

So it was agreed. The four brothers helped Punia launch his newly-won canoe. Muli-loa-of-the-Wagging-Tongue eyed it gravely. "It will be a long hard trip for a lone paddler. I could go with you," he offered.

"Not so," Punia answered hastily. "I will take my time and arrive safely. Have no fear. Aloha."

Punia raised his sail and began his trip back across the long salt sea; back to Oahu—home of his parents, home of his Great Roving Uhu.

Punia had seen another island and he had found out one thing: he liked fishing from his own island best!

Originally there was no written Hawaiian language, only a spoken one. Later, when a written form was needed, it was found that all its sounds could be expressed with twelve English letters: five vowels and seven consonants.

The vowels have these sounds:

a (unaccented) as *a* in *above*	i (unaccented) as *y* in *happy*
a (accented) as *a* in *far*	i (accented) as *ee* in *see*
e (unaccented) as *e* in *bet*	o as *o* in *sole*
e (accented) as *ay* in *play*	u as *oo* in *moon*

The consonants have these sounds:

h, k, l, m, n, p as in English
w after *i* and *e* as *v*;
initially and after *a* sometimes as *v*;
otherwise, as in English

Pronunciation follows these rules:

Every syllable ends with a vowel: Wai-a-le-a-le
Every vowel is sounded: Ha-ne-o-o, pa-o-o

In pronouncing combined vowels (ae, ai, au, ei, eu, oi, ou) stress the first vowel and glide to the next. This sometimes gives the effect of a hidden consonant: aia (ai-ya).

Most Hawaiian words accent the next-to-last syllable and alternating preceding syllables: *O-lo-ma-no*

Words containing five syllables are stressed on the first and fourth syllables: *Ku-ku-i-pa-hu*

ae (*a*-e), yes

ahi (*a*-hi), deep-sea tuna caught with very long line

Ahu-a-pau (A-hu-a-*pa*-u), High Chief of Oahu

aia la! (*ai*-a *la*), There! I told you so! See that!

aku (*a*-ku), deep-sea fish caught with pole and line; bonito

akua (a-*ku*-a), god or spirit

Akua-of-the-Swollen-Billows, a sea kupua killed by Ka-ui-lani

Ala-na-po (A-la-na-*po*), temple of the gods; birthplace of Palila

Alea-wai (A-*le*-a-*wa*-i), section of Hana where Aiai grew up

aloha (a-*lo*-ha), word of greeting or farewell

Anahola (A-na-*ho*-la), mountain ridge pierced by Kapunohu

Apiki (A-*pi*-ki), deceitful; name of one who tricked Pikoi into breaking the Queen's kapu

aumakua (*au*-ma-*ku*-a), family or personal god

auwe! (*a*-u-*we*), alas!

awa (*a*-wa), drink made from root of a shrub

aweoweo (a-*we*-o-*we*-o), a big-eyed red fish

elepaio (*e*-le-*pa*-i-o), bird resembling a woodpecker; watched for guidance in selection of a canoe tree

Ewa (*E*-va), district of Oahu; home of Shark Man

hale (*ha*-le), house, shelter

Hamakua (Ha-ma-*ku*-a), district of Hawaii; home of Three Warriors

Hana (*Ha*-na), district of Hana, ruled by Shark Chief

Hana hou! (*Ha*-na-*hou*), Do it again!

Hanalei (Ha-na-*lei*), place where Kapunohu's spear fell

Hane-o-o (*Ha*-ne-o-o), section of Maui

hau (*ha*-u), a tree that spreads horizontally, forming a tangled network of trunks and branches

Haupu Hill (*Ha*-u-*pu* Hill), home of Kauila-the-Dauntless

Hawaii (Ha-*vai*-i or Ha-*wai*-i), home of Kana, the stretching kupua; an island of the Hawaiian chain

Hilo (*Hi*-lo), city on island of Hawaii

Hina (*Hi*-na),

Hina-of-the-Seashore, wife of Ku-ula, god of fishing

Hina-the-Beautiful, mother of Kana and Niheu

hinalea (hi-*na*-le-a), small, brightly colored fish; used as offering to assure birth of a son; demanded by Shark Chief

Hokulani (Ho-ku-*la*-ni), Heavenly Star; chief's daughter who became Pikoi's wife

Ikuwa (I-ku-*wa*), noisy month of October-November

imu (*i*-mu), earth oven used for roasting food; sometimes for roasting man!

ka! (*ka!*), exclamation of disapproval, disappointment; so that's it!

Kaeko (Ka-e-ko), wife of Opele-of-the-Long-Sleeps

Kaelo (Ka-e-lo), month of January-February; a wet month

Kahoolawe (*Ka*-ho-o-*la*-ve), deserted island where Kalae-puni met his death

kahuna (ka-*hu*-na), priest, advisor

Kakuhi-hewa (*Ka*-ku-hi-*he*-va), king of Oahu

Kalae-puni (Ka-*la*-e-*pu*-ni), the boaster

Kalele (Ka-*le*-le), the bold wisher; son of Opele

kalo (*ka*-lo), staple vegetable root of Hawaiian diet used in making poi; today called taro

kamani (ka-*ma*-ni), a low-branching tree with leathery leaves

Kana (*Ka*-na), the stretching kupua

Kani-kaa (Ka-ni-*ka*-a), spirit partner of Kapunohu

kapa (*ka*-pa), bark cloth used for clothing and sleeping covers; today called tapa

kapu (*ka*-pu), something forbidden

Kapunohu (Ka-*pu*-no-*hu*), champion spearsman

Ka-ua (Ka-*u*-a), the rain; name of Aiai's wife

Kauai (Ka-u-*a*-i), westernmost island; home of Kemamo

Kau-hao (Ka-u-*ha*-o), mother of Ka-ui-lani

Kauila (Ka-u-*i*-la), the Dauntless of Haupu Hill, who carried off Hina-the-Beautiful

Ka-ui-lani (Ka-u-i-*la*-ni), who was aided by Talking Spear

Kea-hua (Ke-a-*hu*-a), father of Ka-ui-lani

Keawe-nui (Ke-*a*-ve-*nu*-i), High Chief of Hawaii

keiki (*kei*-ki), child

Keino (*Kei*-no), -the-Timid; friend of Kalele, the bold wisher

Kemamo (Ke-*ma*-mo), the giant slain by Kapunohu

ki (*ki*), plant whose long smooth leaves were used for wrapping or serving food; today called ti

Kipapa-ula (Ki-*pa*-pa-*u*-la), High Chief of Honolulu, father-in-law of Aiai

koa (*ko*-a), a tree whose hard wood is used especially for canoe-making

Koloa (Ko-*lo*-a), boundary of Kemano the giant's territory

Koni-konia (Ko-ni-ko-*ni*-a), chief of Hawaii who married Ku-ula's sister, Sea-Maid-of-the-Corals

Ko-o-lau (Ko-o-*la*-u), home of Olomano

Kukui-pahu (*Ku*-ku-i-*pa*-hu), Chief of Kohala, brother-in-law of Kapunohu

kupua (ku-*pu*-a), supernatural; a shape-shifter or one with magical powers

Ku-ula (Ku-*u*-la), -of-the-Abundant-Sea; god of fishing

lawaia (la-*wai*-a), a professional fisherman

lehua (le-*hu*-a), a native Hawaiian tree growing high in the mountains

Lono (Lo-no), god of growing things

maikai! (*ma*-i-*ka*-i), exclamation of approval; good!

maile (*ma*-i-le), a sweet-scented vine

Mainele (Ma-i-*ne*-le), Pikoi's rival bowman

Makahiki (Ma-ka-*hi*-ki), harvest festival at which early Hawaiians paid taxes to their chief

Makua (Ma-*ku*-a), term of respect for a relative of one's parents' generation or older

Malia (Ma-*li*-a), Maria; name of Opele's first love

malo (*ma*-lo), loincloth of kapa worn by early Hawaiian men and boys

Maui (Ma-u-i), island where Ku-ula and his family were sentenced to death by Shark Chief

Moi (Mo-i), advisor to Kauila-the-Dauntless

Mokupane (Mo-ku-*pa*-ne), advisor to High Chief Keawe-nui

Moloaa (Mo-lo-*a*-a), end of course in Kapunohu's competition with Kemamo

Molokai (Mo-lo-*ka*-i), home of Kauila-the-Dauntless; also home of Great Eel

Muli-loa (*Mu*-li-*lo*-a), the youngest; Muli-loa-of-the-Wagging-Tongue, youngest of four brothers who took Punia to Kauai

Niheu (Ni-*he*-u), younger brother of Kana, the stretching kupua

Niu-lii (Ni-u-*li*-i), chief of Kohala, rival of Kukui-pahu

Oahu (O-*a*-hu), island of Hawaiian chain; home of Chief Ahu-a-pau

Olomano (O-lo-*ma*-no), giant of Ko-o-lau

olona (o-lo-*na*), fiber used in making rope

Onomea (O-no-*me*-a), cliff with arched hole, on Hawaii
Opele (O-*pe*-le), -of-the-Long-Sleeps; father of Kalele
opihi (o-*pi*-hi), limpet found on rocks; a delicacy
pali (*pa*-li), a cliff
Palila (Pa-*li*-la), owner of the flying war club
Panai (Pa-*na*-i), revenge; vengeful follower of Great Eel
paoo (pa-o-o), fish form taken by brothers of Sea Maid
Pa-o-pele (Pa-o-*pe*-le), great warrior in Kukui-pahu's forces
Pawaa (Pa-*wa*-a), Oahu chief; brother-in-law of Pikoi
Pikoi (Pi-*ko*-i), bowman with four magic arrows
poi (*po*-i), staple food of Hawaiians; paste made from pounded kalo root
  mixed with water
Pueo (Pu-*e*-o), Chief Pueo the Owl, defeated by Kalele
Punia-ka-ia (Pu-*ni*-a-ka-*i*-a), Craving-for-Fish; son of Aiai
uhu (*u*-hu), parrot fish; pet of Punia
Uli (*U*-li), sorceress grandmother of Kana and Niheu
ulua (u-*lu*-a), large game fish
Waiakea (Wa-i-a-*ke*-a), paddler who befriended Pikoi
Wai-a-le-a-le (Wai-*a*-le-*a*-le), wife of Kemamo the giant
Waimanu (Wai-*ma*-nu), home of Opele and Kaeko
Waipio (Wai-*pi*-o), deep valley on island of Hawaii
wiliwili (*wi*-li-*wi*-li), native tree that grows near sea level

Bibliography

Beckwith, Martha W. *Hawaiian Mythology*. New Haven: Yale Univ. Press, 1940.

Buck, Peter H. *Arts and Crafts of Hawaii*. Honolulu: Bishop Museum Press, 1957.

Ellis, William. *Journal of William Ellis*. Honolulu: Advertiser Publishing Co. Ltd., 1963. (Reprint of London 1827 edition and Hawaii 1917 edition).

Emerson, Nathaniel B. *Unwritten Literature of Hawaii*. Tokyo: Charles E. Tuttle Co. Inc., 1965.

Feher, Joseph and others. *Hawaii: A Pictorial History*. Honolulu: Bishop Museum Press, 1969.

Fornander, Abraham. *Collection of Hawaiian Antiquities and Folklore*. Honolulu: Bishop Museum Press, 1916–1920.

Handy. E. S. Craighill, and others. *Ancient Hawaiian Civilization*. Tokyo: Charles E. Tuttle Co. Inc., rev. ed. 1965.

Kane, Herbert Kawainui. *Canoes of Polynesia*. Manuscript, 1971. 850 Valley Road, Glencoe, Illinois.

Malo, David. *Hawaiian Antiquities*. Honolulu: Bishop Museum Press, 1951.

Pukui and Elbert. *English-Hawaiian Dictionary*. Honolulu: Univ. of Hawaii Press, 1964; *Hawaiian-English Dictionary*, ibid. 1957.

Rice, William Hyde. *Hawaiian Legends*. Honolulu: Bishop Museum Bulletin 3, second ed. 1923.

Taylor, Clarice B. *Hawaiian Almanac*. Honolulu: Tongg Pub. Co. Ltd., 1957.

Thrum, Thomas G. *Hawaiian Folk Tales*. Chicago: A. C. McClurg & Co., 1907; *More Hawaiian Folk Tales*, ibid., 1923.

Tinker, Spencer W. *Hawaiian Fishes*. Honolulu: Tongg Pub. Co. Ltd., 1944.

Titcomb, Margaret. *Native Use of Fish in Hawaii*. Supplement to Journal of the Polynesian Society, Memoir 29, New Zealand: Avery Press Ltd., 1952.

Westervelt, William D. *Hawaiian Legends of Old Honolulu*. Tokyo: Charles E. Tuttle Co. Inc., 1965.